THE EXODUS PROJECT

A NOVEL BY A.J. ROWE

Grey Wolfe Publishing, LLC
PO Box 1088
Birmingham, Michigan 48009
www.GreyWolfePublishing.com

© 2015 A.J. Rowe
Published by Grey Wolfe Publishing, LLC
www.GreyWolfePublishing.com
All Rights Reserved

FIRST EDITION ISBN: 978-1628280616
SECOND EDITION ISBN: 978-1628281392
Library of Congress Control Number: 2014957464

THE EXODUS PROJECT

A. J. ROWE

Acknowledgements

Thanks to all of my English teachers and mentors for their advice and continued support, including: Barbara Dunham, Alexender Davidson, Brendon Moylan, Justin Manwell, and special thanks to Edward Utter.

CHAPTER ONE

RESCUE

Roy lay on his back in the crow's nest and gazed up at the pulsing stars littering the night sky. Instinctively, he began to map out constellations, as his father taught him many years ago. Roy was sixteen and had attended the Flight Academy since he was eleven. All of it was preparing him for this flight - aboard the *Exodus*. His first voyage across the sky, Roy was both eager and still somewhat frightened.

The *Exodus* crew consisted of mostly novices like Roy; hotheaded youths seeking adventure, fame, and glory. But when nothing spectacular took place on the first day, many retired to their quarters early with dreams of adventure dancing in their heads. The *Exodus,* an older model, was assigned rookie engineers to teach them the basics of flight. Two hundred eager rookies yearned for the adventure to come.

However, *Exodus'* voyage was unlike any other. For the first time, they were sending an airship over the sea. Such an attempt had not been made during the past two hundred years when conventional watercraft was the primary mode of transport. It would still be that way to this day if the drought hadn't come. Over the past ten years, drought and famine had transformed their once thriving land into a vast ocean of sand, drying up all of the lakes and rivers. Many governments fell to pieces, and factions of sky pirates had arisen, terrorizing the remaining population.

Yet the *Exodus* was equipped to handle them. She was a seven-decked ship with dedicated cargo bays, four powerful engines and two massive zeppelin balloons keeping her aloft. The balloons were supplied by twelve main steam cells, enough to keep her airborne for at least three weeks, maybe more. However, despite the efficiency of steam, it also included dangers.

The cells themselves were as large as a grown man. The inside of a steam cell was also incredibly fragile. Within each cell were innumerable gears, cogs, and pipes, pumping steam through it to the zeppelin balloons, keeping *Exodus* aloft. To keep the cell from falling apart, a thick metal casing enclosed the device, making it bulky and heavy.

Aside from her sleek design, she was also plated with the thickest, strongest hull armor just before their departure, and was well stocked with enough mercury rifles to repel hostile invaders. In spite of *Exodus'* advanced technology, Captain Arthur insisted all personnel carried a pistol with them at all times. Roy didn't question his judgment.

For the fifth time that night, Roy raised his spyglass to his eye and looked around the ship. Everything seemed normal until a silver flash of light caught his eye. He focused his scope for a better view. At first, he saw nothing until the spinning blades of an insect-like ornithopter came into focus. It was a small craft, bearing down on them at high speed. He wondered if it had come from Celis, the town from which they had just departed.

Something was wrong. Its starboard engine was spewing black smoke, and its flying pattern was erratic. Upon closer inspection, Roy noticed their starboard micro-steam cells were damaged and was funneling steam at a dangerous rate into the engine. If not repaired quickly, the results could be disastrous.

Snapping the glass closed, he leapt to the ladder and slid down. He hit the deck running, and made his way around the port cell containment. It was the fastest way to the communications control, his intended destination. Starting on deck one, He ran past decks two, three, and four until he arrived at deck five. Each deck consisted of three sections, A, B, and C. The communications actions grid was located in section C.

He flew down the rows of crew quarters to the farthest section of deck five. Flinging open the door, he stepped inside. The communications control room wasn't much; a small desk and wobbly chair, with dozens of red, yellow and green wires strung about. Pushing the chair out of the way, he flipped a few switches, pulled one of the many levers protruding from the mechanism, and heard the device on the deck buzz to life. Raising the microphone to his mouth, he spoke:

"Unknown craft, this is the *Exodus*. Your ship is in danger, respond." His voice cracked at the last word. He was beginning to tense up as he waited for a response. Nothing.

"Unknown craft, respond!" He said it louder, although he wasn't sure if that would help much. He received nothing but static back from the ornithopter. *Their grid must have been damaged.*

Plan B. Roy switched off the communications channel and returned the frequency to match that of the bridge's. Again, the device whirred to life as it made the connection. "Communications grid to the bridge, respond," he said clearly. A response came within seconds.

"Bridge here. Roy, is that you?" It was Captain Arthur, his voice easily recognizable despite the crackle of the mechanism.

"Roy here sir," he responded. "I've spotted an ornithopter on our tail, bearing down fast. She seems to be damaged, sir, and isn't responding to communications. I suggest we slow down to allow them to catch up." There was a pause. The constant drone of the engines began to fade, and the wind died down. They had taken his advice and slowed the ship.

"Roy, get down to cargo bay one." Captain Arthur's voice came through. "See to it that our guests arrive safely."

"Aye, sir. Communications out." Roy closed the channel and made his way down another deck to the cargo bay. The three cargo bays were the only places manned 24/7, besides the bridge. Crewman strode about, carrying heavy boxes to be sorted. Being the first day of their journey, the cargo had not yet been properly stowed. The docking clamp was being used to move things about. Amidst the mess, Roy spotted Ferren Benette, the one member of the crew, besides the captain, with whom he was acquainted.

"I understand we're receiving guests?" Ferren said without even looking up from his clipboard as Roy approached. Ferren was a year older than Roy and a serious minded person when it came to his work, but he actually seemed to have developed a sense of humor while off duty, with Roy's help. Ferren was assigned as the cargo bay chief for their five-day voyage, and while he was a competent worker, he was slow.

"Yeah," Roy replied. "The captain asked me to help you clear landing space."

"Indeed." Ferren continued to scribble on his clipboard. He then turned to a small operating deck higher up. "Ready the clamp for docking procedures!" he instructed. "Clear landing dock three of all cargo, and open the bay doors!"

The crew responded quickly, clearing out the cargo and revealing a series of small circular slots, designed to stabilize any craft in the cargo bay if they encountered turbulence. The massive clamp moved into position as the bay doors rose slowly. Roy's brown hair rippled as they were buffeted by the wind. The ornithopter was much closer now; close enough to make out two figures perched at the helm. The first, a taller man adorned with pilot's gear, sat calmly at the wheel. The second, a short figure in a white coat and goggles strode nervously back and forth behind the pilot. His mouth was moving rapidly, and his arms in angry gestures.

The lights on the landing dock lit up the night, and the craft made a beeline for it. The smoke billowing from the engine had thickened, and the engine coughed and sputtered. Her landing struts extended and the graceful wings folded into the ship. Her hull reflected the red flash of the landing lights as it began to clear the bay doors. The landing clamp extended and latched on to her hull. She was stable.

Then, without warning, their engine gave a final cough and blew. A flurry of sparks showered down from it as it tumbled sideways into the side of the bay door. The landing clamp bent, and its wooden frame splintered as the ornithopter was ripped from its grasp. There was another explosion as its starboard steam cells ruptured, and it fell back out of the bay, tumbling through the night sky. The *Exodus* lurched from the impact, and piles of unsecured cargo came down; the crew scrambled to avoid them. Roy and Ferren were both thrown off their feet and hit the deck hard.

They looked over at each other and locked eyes for a moment. They knew they both had the same idea. They scrambled to their feet and ran over to the small communications array in the back of the bay. Ferren opened the channel, and Roy snatched up the microphone. He didn't have to say anything before a message came through.

"What's going on down there?" Captain Arthur's voice cracked through the device.

"The copter's engines just blew, sir," Roy said. "She's falling fast, five o'clock."

The *Exodus* swung about and her engines roared to life. Roy could see the ornithopter through the bay doors. At least half of the micro-steam cells had ruptured on her starboard side, spewing broken pieces of machinery into the engine.

"We aren't going fast enough!" Ferren yelled over the roar of the engines. "We won't catch up with them!"

"Grappling hooks?" Roy recommended, but Ferren shook his head.

"We have too much forward velocity," he said. "They wouldn't get enough range."

Roy thought for a while, before saying quietly, "I would."

"Don't be stupid," Ferren growled. "There's got to be another option."

Roy ignored him and returned to the communications array. The channel was still open to the bridge. "Captain, I'm going after them." He spoke clearly into the microphone; his pulse intensified.

"Absolutely not." The captain's voice came, although even through the distorted frequency, he could hear some doubt in his own voice.

"Captain, it's the only way. There are two people on that craft, and they'll both die without my help. Please, sir."

The microphone crackled. The captain had sighed. "Under normal circumstances, I would never let you do this."

"These are hardly normal circumsta-"

"Go!" he barked. "And don't tell your mother I let you do this!"

Roy didn't try to suppress his grin. Even in times like this, their stubborn, fearless captain could have a sense of humor. "Aye, sir!" He closed the channel.

Roy took hold of a clip hanging from the wall and latched it to his belt. A small sign by the reel read '200 feet'. *I've got 200 feet to reach the falling ship. Any more and the rope will go taught, and I will have failed.* A sudden panic ran through him.

What if the rope breaks? What if I don't reach it in time? Stupid thoughts.

"Wait, wait, wait!" Ferren said, trying to yank him off the platform extending out the bay doors. "You'll die from the impact!"

"If I'm only moving just a little bit faster than the ship, it will be like walking on air." Roy pushed him back and turned to face the clouds whipping by. He closed his eyes, held his breath, and jumped.

Chapter Two
Lester Fitzroy

The wind whipped Roy's clothes around him. Everything was spinning; the rope holding him was slack. He couldn't determine which direction was up, or down. His lungs weren't functioning properly; he couldn't breathe. Below him, he saw a spinning spec getting closer and closer—the ornithopter. He pulled his arms tight to his sides and loosened his legs to absorb the impact. He hadn't put on wind goggles, so it was difficult to see between rapid blinks.

His speed increased, and the aircraft came into view. He was able to make out the man in the white coat clinging to the railing like his life depended on it, but the pilot was nowhere to be seen. Roy took hold of his rope and pulled himself up so he was falling feet first. Despite his theory about hitting the deck softly, he was still going considerably faster than the copter. He let his knees slack and closed his eyes.

Wham!

Roy hit the deck rolling head over heels. Once, twice, three times over before he came to a stop. He inhaled deeply, his lungs functioning once again. His bearings were still completely lost, however. The world tilted to the left, then suddenly back to the right. He wasn't sure if this was a result of his own disorientation or the movement of the damaged craft. He managed to pull himself to his feet.

The man in the white coat was bent over the wheel but was making no attempt to stabilize the craft. He was crouched over a lifeless figure slumped over the controls. The man in the coat was taking his pulse. After a few seconds of doing so, he sighed and shook his head. He straightened, and turned to the deck as if to accept his fate. Then he saw Roy.

The man was an older person, with pale skin, a large pale spot atop his head, and sunken eyes. He wasn't a robust person, yet his facial features seemed like they had been crammed on to his head, with caterpillar eyebrows and a wrinkled nose. *I wonder what it looks like when he frowns*, Roy thought.

"Wha-" he said, shocked. "How did you get here?"

"No time to explain!" Roy ran up to him and began to tie the slack rope around the man's waist.

"We're going up?!" he asked, not hiding the fear in his voice. "You can't be serious! Can the rope support all of our weight?"

"It's either that or be incinerated when the steam cells blow, make your choice."

The man pursed his lips and strode back and forth in anxiety. "All of my supplies are here... I can't give them up!"

"You're going to have to," Roy said, switching to a sympathetic tone of voice in an attempt to get him to move faster. "I'm sorry."

The man eventually stopped pacing and allowed Roy to finish tethering him around the waist. There wasn't much slack left in the rope, and the *Exodus* was growing farther and farther away. As he finished, a loud whistling began to fill the air. The steam had made its way into the engine. They only had a few seconds.

"Come on!" Roy began to lead the man towards the railing of the craft. He rattled off in protest, but Roy ignored him. They reached the rail, and without listening to a word the man was saying, he placed a hand on his back and pushed him over the edge. He squealed in fright as he tumbled off the edge of the ship, and Roy followed close behind.

As soon as his feet cleared the railing, the steam contaminating the engines gave off a spark. Just one spark: and the entire ship blew. All twelve of their micro-steam cells ruptured at once, and the explosion sent them both reeling, clinging to the rope for their lives. The man watched with eyes full of sadness as all of his cargo was incinerated along with the copter.

For a long time after that, as they were slowly reeled back onto the ship like helpless fish caught on a line, the man was silent. Roy was too; although, on the inside, he was bursting with pride. He just saved a life that day, something many young flight academy graduates yearn for. He was a hero.

Finally, the man spoke up. "I suppose I owe you a debt of gratitude." Roy didn't notice before how official and calm his voice was, despite all that had just taken place. "What might your name be?"

"Roy," he replied, extending his hand to shake until he realized they were several feet apart. He awkwardly let it drop to his side. "Roy Mulleary."

"Lester Fitzroy." the man said, and then added, "Doctor Lester Fitzroy."

"Doctor?" Roy asked. "A medical doctor?"

"No, I have a Ph.D. in archeology. Of course, I'm a medical doctor!"

Roy was rather taken aback by his sudden anger until he remembered that all of the doctor's belongings were just incinerated. The doctor obviously realized this and sighed.

"I apologize," he murmured. "All of my medical supplies were on that ship. I wouldn't suppose you have any on board?"

"Very little," Roy admitted. "Where were you heading?"

"Well, I'm about fifty feet from my intended destination now," the doctor said, adjusting the tight rope around his waist, wincing slightly. "I was assigned to the *Exodus* as chief officer of medical practices. Unfortunately, I missed the flight. It took half the day to find a pilot to take me here and another half day just to get here." He wasn't trying to hide the annoyance in his voice. "During our journey, however, we were attacked by pirates. We fought back, but we were no match for their heavy weapons. Our hull armor crumpled like paper, and our starboard engine took a direct blast. We resorted to desperate measures and dumped kerosene into the functional engine. The fumes it produced severely damaged the pirates' means of propulsion and they were forced to withdraw."

"Dump kerosene into the engines..." Roy murmured. "An excellent idea."

The doctor beamed with pride. "Of course it is! I came up with it myself, after all."

Slowly, the voices up above came into range as they cleared the last few feet of their climb. The captain was there. Lacking a very muscular form, he pulled a couple cadets aside to help the doctor and Roy up.

"Outstanding work, boy!" Arthur boomed in a voice that didn't quite match the captain's stature as Roy was hoisted aboard. "I'll see to it that this ship becomes your permanent assignment if it's the last thing I do." He then turned to the doctor and shook his hand. The tone of their voices suggested they had met before.

Many of the crew congratulated Roy on his outstanding actions as he made his way to find Ferren. When he found him, Roy noticed that his fingernails were bitten down so far that they oozed blood. Although he expressed no special regards to him when they found each other, Roy knew that he was secretly terrified of losing his friend.

"I'd say this calls for a celebration!" The captain's voice boomed about the cargo bay. "To the mess hall!" A rousing cheer went up among the crew. As strong-willed a person as the captain was, he always looked for an excuse to have a party. Ferren and Roy decided to take the long way around to deck two, where the mess hall was located, to avoid the swarm of crewmen eager for something to eat, despite it being nearly five o'clock in the morning.

When they arrived, they found the dining area in no different condition than it usually was, aside from the fact that it was quickly filling with cadets. The smell of liquor and coffee filled the air. The captain loved his drinks. The dining stewardess called the two over to the counter.

"What can I getcha, sugar?" the stewardess, Emily, asked them with a wink, leaning her thin elbow on the countertop.

'Sugar' was her nickname for every one of the male gender aboard the ship, and seeing as she was the only girl aboard, this meant everyone. Emily was a year older than Roy, Ferren's age and had floated from ship to ship as a dining stewardess ever since she could hold a plate. She was dressed in all black with white lining at the edges of her sleeves and skirt, and always wore an excessive amount of dark makeup. She had dark red curly hair, and never wore jewelry. She once remarked that it just gets in the way, although it was also likely she didn't own any. Working as a stewardess yielded little pay.

"Two cups of coffee, please." Roy requested, and Emily turned and strode back into the kitchen, her shoulder length curls bobbing. He noticed that Ferren's cheeks had gone scarlet red for a moment. Despite Ferren's technical smarts, he was not good with socializing.

"I do not," Ferren said, running his hands through his hair, "Understand the purpose of drinking at five o'clock in the morning."

"Aww, c'mon!" Roy clapped him on the shoulder. "It's a celebration! Have some fun with it!"

Emily returned with two steaming coffees with bits of chocolate shavings dotting the surface. "First round's on the captain," she said when Roy reached into his pocket to pay, and then added in a low murmur, "I imagine he'll pay for just about anybody's rounds today, so don't expect to have to pay much."

"Noted." Ferren said, and they went to find a seat. The captain caught his eye.

"Roy!" The captain called. "Over here!"

"Of course, of course..." the captain was saying. "You have my permission to use any of the medical supplies you can find here, and section C of deck six for your medical bay." His cheeks were flushed a rosy red. *Was he already drunk?*

"Thank you, captain." The doctor nodded in thanks, the electric light reflecting off his shiny head.

Roy used the small spoon in his coffee to scoop up the cream and chocolate shavings. Such a luxury wasn't available where he once lived. If you wanted a coffee, you had to go to the market, buy a bag of coffee beans, grind it up, and pour it into a cup of steaming water. It was usually incredibly dry and bitter in taste.

Roy had lived in one of the last places on the continent that could be considered civilized. It wasn't the largest town, but everyone relied on each other. They had no currency or forms of money. They simply traded goods with one another, and Roy never thought twice about it until he joined the flight academy. The first day there, he brought a small bag of coffee beans with which to pay for his meals. After he realized that it wouldn't be accepted, an older boy offered to pay for his meal. That was Ferren.

As enticing as his drink was, however, a more serious detail crossed his mind that he had forgotten about. He turned to Doctor Fitzroy. "Doctor," Roy said. "May I ask you something?"

"I'm all ears." The doctor leaned back in his chair and eyed him with a certain curiosity. Roy wasn't sure if he should feel safe or stalked under that look.

"The pirates, doctor," Roy said quickly. "You said you disabled them?"

"Yes, quite brilliantly if I say so myself." The doctor beamed.

"But are they still out there?"

The doctor's pride faded ever so slightly. "Well... Yes, I would suppose so." He shrugged as if it were the most trivial matter in the world.

"Could it be possible they were coming for us? For the *Exodus*?"

"I... suppose it's a possibility." The doctor frowned. "But that would mean an organized attack – are pirates even capable of that?"

"You mentioned that their weapons were able to pierce your hull armor like it was paper. Could you describe them a little more?"

"It all happened so fast..." murmured the doctor. "I think they were explosive based. Launched like mortars. Our armor buckled like tin foil under the fire."

"How large were the ships?"

The doctor thought for a moment, his face contorting in thought. "Not much larger than the craft I arrived on. Small zeppelins, I would say. Single ballooned, two engines. The usual equipment for a standard traveling ship, besides the weapons."

The captain was listening intently on their conversation, one eyebrow raised. "If they return," he said, clenching his fist. "We'll be ready."

"Captain, permission to begin work on a—"

"—Defense against the mortars. Yes, please do." Captain Arthur finished as if reading his mind. "Doctor, unless you have sick to attend to, I would like you to work with Roy."

"Captain!" Doctor Fitzroy was shocked. "I'm a doctor, not an engineer! I wouldn't know the first thing about hull modific-!"

"You are also the only eyewitness we have on those weapons." The captain cut him off, and when the doctor opened his mouth in protest, he added, "That's an order."

Lester Fitzroy sat for a while, considering the offer. "Aye aye, sir." He said finally. "May I request a night's sleep first, however? It's been a long journey."

"Of course. You and Roy can begin work on the hull at ten o'clock sharp tomorrow morning. And doctor, I recommend a change of clothes as well. That coat will be ruined. Dismissed."

Chapter Three

Pursuit

Roy awoke at the nine o'clock morning Bell. The skies were densely clouded that morning, hindering their sight. In the event of sight deprivation like this, it was required that engines be cut to half power in case an emergency stop had to be performed. From the hum of the engines, Roy could tell that the requirement had been met. He got up and made his way to the mess hall for a late breakfast.

Emily was serving hot, fluffy pancakes with a rich syrup on the side. She slid a plate with a stack of steaming pancakes before him. "Eat up." She said, setting the small pitcher of syrup beside his plate. Roy nodded his thanks and emptied the pitcher over the fluffy goodness. It tasted like liquid gold. As he stuffed his mouth, he secretly hoped that the captain was serious about having him serve a permanent position aboard the *Exodus*. A life aboard a ship of exploration was his dream, despite everyone's recommendation to register on ships like the *Dauntless*, or *Yorktown*; ships made for battle. He couldn't help but think that cadets aboard ships like those were expendable. He remembered the day the *Dauntless* was commissioned in his hometown. It was made with the latest in flight-ready weaponry: Gatling guns, cannons, mortars... only the best of the time.

The thought of weaponry reminded him that he had work to do. He quickly finished his pancakes, piled the dishes on the counter, and began to make his way out of the mess hall. As he left, doctor Fitzroy was just entering. He wore an engineer's uniform, the clips and buckles all undone. He walked stiffly as if every movement caused him discomfort. "There you are!" the doctor said. "You were supposed to meet me at ten o'clock come on!"

"What time is it now?" Roy asked as the doctor dragged him along, thinking he might have overslept.

"Six past the hour! Now, come on!" Roy increased to a steady jog to keep up with the stout doctor.

They went up to deck three, where the main armor plating was located. The cargo bay there contained their spare steam cells, which was why it was the most heavily armored deck on the ship. If one of those blew, the *Exodus* journey would come to a rather fiery end.

"What type of armor was the ornithopter equipped with?" Roy asked as he pulled a lever on the wall. A locker clanked open and he looked through the supplies within, roping both a wrench and a mallet to his belt.

"I have no idea," the doctor said flatly. "I'm a doctor. I never went to flight school. I fact, I never even-"

"Looks. Thickness, size, details. What did it look like?" Roy interrupted, tossing the doctor a screwdriver. He fumbled with it and dropped it.

"Well..." he murmured, bending over and snatching up the screwdriver. "It wasn't very thick, but it was curved up at the bottom. Lined with a brighter kind of metal, I'm not sure what, exactly. There were twelve plates in all, one for each steam cell."

"Curved up, about the size of a micro-steam cell..." Roy tried to recall his days in the academy. He had frequent tests much like this, and it was almost like a pop quiz for him. "Probably type four," he concluded, pulling on wind goggles. He also tossed a pair to the doctor. "We are equipped with type fives. If your armor didn't stand a chance, neither will ours."

The doctor wasn't paying any attention to him. He was trying to adjust the goggles to fit over his eyes. His eyes were relatively close together, and the goggles were wide on his small head. "These are horrendous!" he exclaimed. "They're so scratched up I can't see a thing out of them! I demand a better pair." He wrenched them off his head and held them out to Roy.

"Those are the best ones we've got, doc." Roy didn't touch the goggles in the doctor's hand, but instead closed and locked the wall locker. The doctor blinked, obviously not expecting that response. Probably out of shock, he put the goggles back on wordlessly. Roy triumphantly led him to the edge of the deck, just above the hull plating.

"That looks a lot like ours," the doctor said innocently, wrinkling his nose under the pressure of the stiff goggles.

"That's because it is," Roy said simply. "Three-quarters of an inch thicker, two feet wider and three longer. Very similar to yours indeed."

"Got any ideas?"

"I was thinking," Roy said. "You said the mortars seemed to go right through your armor?"

"I do think so."

"They must have been sharp-headed to do that kind of damage," Roy said, running his hand over the sleek steel of the armor, thinking. He remembered playing with an air rifle his father got him for his birthday one year. He used an old tin pan as his target, and within two years, it could have been mistaken for scrap metal. He also filled the surrounding wall with holes. The pellets would glance off the pot when he hit it at an angle, doing little damage.

"How about..." Roy murmured, leaning over the edge to get a better view of the clamps holding the plating tight against the hull. One could easily be modified to extend out a foot or so, resulting in slanted hull armor. It was so simple, and yet incredibly effective. "Hold this," Roy commanded, thrusting the wrench into the doctor's hands. He walked over to the cargo bay communications grid and opened a channel to the bridge. There was a moment of static as the microphone buzzed on.

"Bridge here;" came a bridge crewman's voice.

"Could you put the captain on?"

"Sure thing." There was some static for a moment before a strong voice boomed through the system.

"Captain here," Arthur said.

"Captain, it's Roy," he said. "I think I've got an idea for a defense modification, sir. I'll need seven repair crews, one for each deck. I know it's a lot, sir, but with enough work, we'll be done before the day's end; Sir."

"Get on it. I'm putting you in charge of coordinating the teams." The captain didn't hesitate with his answer. "Ops has picked up faint radio transmissions far behind. Someone's out there."

"Understood." Roy closed the channel, and within twenty seconds, a ship - wide announcement came over the speaker.

"Attention, repair teams one through seven report to deck three immediately. I repeat, repair teams one through seven report to deck three immediately." The captain's voice was indefinite. "You will be working around the clock until this job is finished, so the sooner, the better. Get to work!"

Doctor Fitzroy tapped Roy on the shoulder. "Umm, excuse me," he said timidly. "I wouldn't happen to be in one of these repair teams? So, if you'll excuse me, I'll-

"You are now." Roy caught him by the arm as he attempted to flee. "Group four, I reckon, should need some extra help. Get to it."

"Who put you in charge?" The doctor returned, looking Roy up and down as if sizing him up.

"The captain told me specifically to coordinate these teams." Roy crossed his arms over his chest. "Move it!"

The repair crews reported in to Roy. Seventy of them total, ten per group. They all seemed eager to get the job done and take a nap. The doctor joined the fourth repair team following an onslaught of protests, but finally complied in the end. Roy distributed the assignments, and within the hour, they were all at work on the hull.

His idea was to attach a pressurized hydraulic to the second clamp holding the armor tight against the hull. At a moment's notice, the entire process would take seventeen seconds, Roy predicted, the modifications could be activated with the crank of a lever, and the ship would unfurl its new defenses. With luck, it should be enough to glance the mortars off the hull, giving them the extra time they needed to stop the ships' advance.

They greased their tools, pulled on their coats and set to work. The captain broke protocol and increased engines to maximum output to buy them the time they needed. Roy stayed on deck three in the cargo bay and helped Ferren find old hydraulics in storage.

"What do you think about this whole thing?" Roy asked Ferren, his hands covered in grease, as he separated out hydraulics from old spare components.

"This whole thing?" Ferren said in his usual, emotionless voice. "I'm not sure I know what you mean."

"I mean our situation. Do you think we'll be overpowered? Killed?"

"Way to think optimistically," Ferren murmured with a hint of sarcasm, then added, "I should hope that we won't be attacked at all, as slim of a chance it may seem. You?"

"I don't know. I mean, I want to continue living and all, but a part of me almost wants to-"

"A part of you?" Ferren interrupted. "Your body functions as a whole. What 'part of you' wants to do anything?"

Roy chuckled. Ferren's social skills didn't include slang phrases either. "A part of me. Inside. A background thought if you will."

Ferren stopped for a moment, processing the information. His eyebrows rose, and he shrugged. "Go on," he said simply, returning to his task.

"...Anyways, deep down inside, I want to hope that we'll be attacked. I'd like some action, and an excuse to try out those rifles. Mercury powered, ought to be fun."

Ferren sighed and turned to face Roy. "I will never understand your unnatural lust for potentially life threatening scenarios. You've had enough 'action' for the next week, with your escapade involving the doctor's rescue."

Roy laughed out loud. "You have a long way to go, friend," he said, and handed a handful of hydraulics to a few waiting engineers. "Hop to it," he commanded sternly. The cadets actually jumped a little, before scurrying off to do their work with a few mumbles of "Yessir." They had a sudden respect for him - almost as if trying to impress him. His actions the day before had obviously earned him a reputation. Ironic, really, that they had no idea he was the same rank as they.

Roy stood and examined his work. Two large crates full of usable hydraulics. That was easily enough to refit the ship. He pulled off his utility belt, setting it aside.

"Going somewhere?" Ferren said dryly. He was still sifting through the crates of equipment.

"As a matter of fact, yes," Roy said. "And you're coming with me."

"I," Ferren started. "Have plenty a place to be that could be much more beneficial to this ship and it's its crew, that doesn't include you."

Roy had learned to not be offended by that. He wasn't trying to be insulting, rather, he was just giving it to him logically. "Think of it as your training," Roy said, pulling Ferren to his feet and walking him over to the cargo bay weapons locker. He opened it to find four shining, greased rifles staring back at him.

"You cannot be serious." Ferren backed away. "We are not going to shoot guns at each other at a time like this."

"We aren't going to," Roy assured him, pulling out two rifles and tossing one to Ferren. Roy had longed to hold one, and now was his chance.

"I will not fire this," Ferren said simply, attempting to push the weapon back into Roy's hands.

"We aren't firing blasts!" Roy said, pulling back on the silver lever next to the gun's chamber. A small pack of five mercury blasts fell out. "We're using mock rounds," he explained, jamming a new set of blasts into the mechanism. Instead of shiny, brass heads, they were armed with a light covering of rubber filled with clay. The mock rounds fired small clusters of clay balls formed by the explosion of the gun. They were non-lethal, but could still leave a bruise.

"I still refuse to fire this at you." Ferren insisted. "It is an unnecessary risk of injury."

"Well, the *Exodus* is equipped with a prototype target practice system," Roy remarked, remembering the ship schematics he saw during his academy days. "Why not try it out?"

A slight fire of anticipation flashed in Ferren's eyes for just a moment before he returned to his usual self. He bit his lip, his gaze flashing between the rifle and floor. "I... Suppose I could use the extra training."

"That's just what I thought." Roy clapped him on the shoulder, and with the other hand, pulled a lever labeled 'training sequence'. There were some loud clanks as machinery settled into place for the first time. Ferren loaded the mock rounds and they took their place by the rail under the hull armor.

Roy raised the weapon to his side. It fit snugly under the crook of his shoulder. His thumb pulled back on the hammer and a sight flipped up at the end of the long barrel. He waited a few seconds. There was a clank, and a small target was freed from the hull and snatched up by the wind. Roy lined up the sights, but before his finger could close around the trigger, there was crack beside him and the target spiraled off into the clouds.

Roy stared at Ferren as he calmly lifted the rifle and pulled back on the silver ball. A blast casing was ejected from the mechanism, and another fresh round was slid into the barrel. "Not bad..." Roy murmured, and they again lifted their rifles. Another target was released, and Roy fired without hesitation. The target spun off.

"Ha!" Roy blurted, lowering the weapon. "How's that?"

"Impressive," Ferren remarked. "But-"

There was a sharp clang on metal in the distance.

They both froze. That noise hadn't come from the *Exodus*, but from out beyond the ship. They slowly turned to look at each other. Another target was loosed on a clockwork timer, and this time, neither of them tried to shoot it down. They waited a few seconds. Another clang. There was only one thing that could be making that noise. Another ship.

CHAPTER FOUR

ASSAULT

Roy scrambled to the communications grid and frantically opened a channel to the main bridge, deck one. "Captain! Captain, do you read?" he cried into the microphone. He received no reply but static. The ship must have been projecting a signal disruptor in the direction of their ship, and now that the targets being released left a trail of their location, they could no longer hide. Disruptor signals were impossible to detect unless you specifically scanned for one, which they had no reason to do. Until now.

"We've got to get to the bridge," Ferren said, his usual seriousness returning. "If we can alter our course, we might get out of the range of the disruptor signal.

"Agreed," Roy said, trying to stay as serious as Ferren, but he found it incredibly difficult. He was never quite certain how he managed to remain so calm all the time. "I'll get to the bridge, you get those modifications working."

Ferren turned on his heel and began barking orders to the engineers. They scrambled to obey. Meanwhile, Roy made his way around the outer hull plating and began to climb the rigging. A quicker way up, but not entirely stable. Step by step, he climbed like a flea clinging to the hide of some wild beast. As much of a fortress as the *Exodus* was, without those hull modifications activated, they didn't stand a chance.

He was about halfway past deck two when he began to hear the whine of an unfamiliar engine. It wasn't the *Exodus*, and it was soon joined by another. They were closing in like hawks coming in for the kill, their prey completely unsuspecting of the impending attack He was almost at the bridge, and he hurried his climbing. *If they opened fire now, I would be tossed from the hull like a rag doll.*

There must have been others who noticed the ships by now as well, but must have encountered the same problem. With their signal broken, there was no form of communicating it to the bridge. Roy could see the scratched glass windows surrounding the bridge, and shadowed figures moving within. They had no idea of what was to come.

Roy took hold of the windowsill and pulled himself up, rapping on the window with his palm, but the sound was snatched away by the wind and engine roars. He clenched his fist and punched it. Hard. Still nothing. Sighing, he slung the rifle off his shoulder and brought the stock down on the window. The glass shattered inward, and Roy fell in with it. After recovering from the initial shock, he noticed that the entire bridge crew was staring at him. The captain, at the helm, recovered first.

"Mulleary!" he barked. "What the hell are you-"

"Captain, adjust our course!" Roy blurted, standing up out of the glass shards. "Ninety degrees starboard! We're caught in a disruptor signal, sir. Those ships are almost on us!"

Captain Arthur understood quickly. He flipped up the small astrolabe beside the helm and brought the wheel around to match the ninety-degree mark. The ship swung around to comply, and, without warning, the communications grid began spewing gibberish. Every grid on every deck available must have been in use, desperately trying to reach one another.

"Terminate the links," the captain ordered, and the man at the grid closed the channels. "Reopen a single channel, ship-wide broadcast."

The engineer complied, and the ship-wide broadcast whistle sounded. "All hands to battle stations!" the captain roared. "Activate the hull modifications, whether they're ready or not! All decks, begin armament distribution to all personnel!"

Even from the bridge, the commotion could be heard. The slam of machinery being powered up, the clank of rifles handed out to the engineers, the roar of the engines. And with the captain's order, the *Exodus* opened up to her full potential like a great bird unfurling its wings for the first time as the ships came into view.

There were two of them, nowhere close to the fortress sized hull of the *Exodus*, but still armed to the teeth. At least two mortar launchers were easily spotted on the first ship's main deck, and one on the second. They were both adorned with the scarlet and navy blue colors that were almost universally recognized as pirate symbols. As the *Exodus* revealed her newfound defenses, the pursuers actually seemed to hesitate, as if dismayed by her, but they soon broke off a pursuit course and assumed a common attack pattern, one ship approaching starboard and the other port. They were both double decked, single ballooned ships, heavily armed with thick plating crudely strapped to the hull. *Pirates*, Roy thought.

"Fire at will!" The captain bellowed into the main communications grid on the bridge, and within seconds, the crew complied. Shots rang out throughout the decks, and the sound of blast casings clattering to the ground followed suit. Roy could see the flashes of light the silvery blasts traced across the skyline as they embedded themselves in the ships' hull. The pirate ships rocked in the sky but were up un-damaged. Their hull was holding.

Then the pirates opened fire.

The sound of mortar fire was heard by everyone on the ship when they began. The port ship, the one armed with two launchers, fired first. Roy held his breath as the massive mortar shell, the size of a small boy, whistled towards the hull, but it was misfired. It sailed far below the *Exodus*, falling short and disappearing in the clouds. The ship to their starboard fired as well, but it also came short.

"They're firing warning shots," Roy warned. "They misfired on purpose."

"Good observation, cadet," the captain said gruffly, but whether he was being sarcastic or not escaped him. "They think we'll stand down!" Even if the captain thought they wouldn't stand down, many of the crew did. The gunfire rattling out throughout the decks became thinned and fewer. They were hesitating. The captain noticed as well. Taking hold of the microphone in the communications grid, he yelled into it. "I don't care what they threaten you with, keep firing until our ammunition stores run dry and our knives are dulled and broken! Understood!"

The weapons fire increased. The crew, encouraged by their captain's stern willed strategy, opened fire again. The blasts rattled off and the pirates loosed another volley, but it too came short. This time, the crew didn't hesitate to return fire.

The pirates now knew that the crew of the *Exodus* meant business. They raised their sights and lined up the hull with them. Three more shots blew off, only this time, they weren't warning shots. "Let's hope those modifications work..." Roy murmured to himself. His grip on the windowsill tightened. *Now or never.* The shells whistled closer. The weapons fire aboard the *Exodus* ceased as the crew took cover. Roy bit his lip until it began to bleed.

The first shell struck the hull plating directly, and after a moment of terror, they were flooded with relief. The ship was rocked a bit, but the shell didn't detonate. Instead, it glanced off the slanted armor and spiraled down through the clouds. The other two shells did the same.

A rallying cry went up among the decks as they rained a storm of blasts on the approaching ships. The armor was holding, but for how long was anybody's guess. They began to drop astern, but not in retreat. They adjusted their sights to match.

"They're trying to concentrate fire," Roy observed. The captain ordered evasive maneuvers to compensate, but the pirates' aim was not thrown. Three more shots rang out and all three were deflected like a blade on a shield. The ship rocked dangerously, and how much longer it would last was anybody's guess. "Captain, let me go down there." Roy requested, sliding his thumb under the strap of the rifle. "I need to help our assault teams."

"I don't recall admitting you up here in the first place!" The captain said with a grin. "Get down there!"

Roy, instead of using the rigging again, strode to the hatch at the front of the bridge. Flinging it open, he began to descend the main ladder. The convenient thing about the main ladder was that it went all the way through the ship, making transport for units off of the bridge quick and easy. When he reached the cargo bay on deck three, he hopped down off the ropes and ran across the deck, ducking under the rail beside another gun-wielding engineer. Roy drew his pistol and aimed it over the rail, bringing only his eye level out of the safety of cover. He switched the safety off and pulled the trigger.

Blast casings rained down on Roy and his comrades as they hammered the ships with gunfire. The ships had drawn even closer, concentrating their fire on a set of hull armor plating not far from their location. Shell after shell they fired, rocking the *Exodus* dangerously, but not enough to bring her down. Roy dared a peek down at the heavily fired upon section. His stomach flopped as he inhaled quickly at the sight. The armor plating was heavily damaged, and the makeshift hydraulic was beginning to split. It hissed as precious pressurized air was released from the device, and the armor slowly began to flatten out to its original position.

"Ferren!" Roy cried over the battle and saw a head look up over the sea of people. It was him, and from a special skill only best of friends could achieve, they communicated to each other what was happening. They knew. Ferren stood and began barking to the engineers there, ordering them to evacuate. Many complied while others stayed to finish off a full clip's worth of ammunition.

"Move!" Roy tried to pull the rebellious cadets to their feet, but they wouldn't budge. Another shell crashed into the weakened section of the hull, and while it successfully reflected the shot, the hydraulic snapped and hung crooked off a broken angle. The plating fell to the side with it. The cargo bay was completely open to attack.

"Come on!" Ferren, with a surprising strength, yanked the cadet to his feet and pulled him along. Roy did the same with another, and they made for the rigging to deck four. He heard the boom of a shell being fired. They had seconds. Ferren made it up the rigging in time. Roy and the cadet were next, and they barely had a hold of the ropes when the shell hit right on target. There was an explosion behind them, and black smoke blinded and choked them. Roy opened his eyes to see that the cadet was no longer beside him. He frantically looked around for him, only to see his hand desperately clutching the last of the rigging ropes. Roy tried to make his way down to him, wheezing from the smoke.

His face was contorted with fear. Blood poured from a gash across his chest, sapping the life from him. Roy reached down with his free hand to help him.

The cadet looked up and locked eyes with Roy for just a moment.

He fell.

"NO!" Roy screamed his throat raw as his body became a spec in his vision and was gone. Roy tore at the ropes in frustration. A burning heat seared within him while the fires began to singe his skin. Deck three was in flames, and not much was left beside splinters. Two more explosions rattled off, and Roy almost fell to the same fate as the fallen cadet. He leaped from rope-to-rope, but he wasn't going to deck four. He passed by it on his way down.

When he finally reached deck six, he dropped off the rigging and made his way around the lookout point, his favorite place to be aboard the *Exodus*, and it was in flames. He had passed by his destination the day before on his way to the cargo bay. *There!* The steam containment cells were located at the far side of deck six. There were twelve massive containers total, each containing enough steam to last days. But flying wasn't what Roy had in mind for them.

He made his way to the containment controls and scanned it for anything resembling an eject system. A large red lever labeled *emergencies only* was easily found. *Well*, he thought. *This is certainly an emergency.* Hit pulled the lever out. A hissing sound loud enough to wake the dead filled the deck, and the ship began to rock unsteadily, but not from mortar fire. Below each of the steam cells, another lever resembling the one Roy just pulled jutted out from a small contraption. He made his way over to the one located farthest astern and slid the rifle off his shoulder. *I'm going to deploy them like missiles.*

He grasped the handle beneath the cell. Holding it firmly, he leaned over the edge of the ship and looked back at their attackers. The two ships were beginning to cross around to even out the damage done. He waited. The larger and more powerful of the two ships was falling behind the smaller one to take a different front of attack. *Any second now*, Roy thought, his knuckles white on the lever.

The ships were aligned. Without hesitation, he heaved on the lever. It didn't move. Dumbfounded, Roy looked down at the lever. The bolt holding it in place was damaged by the attack, and no longer attached to the emergency release. Roy swore under his breath. *I need to get it loose!* He thought.

He searched around for something - anything to get it free. His hand found his belt, where a single pistol blast resided. It wasn't entirely compatible with the mercury rifles, but it should still fire. He pulled the silver ball back and opened the loading chamber. It was sealed tight due to the fact that there was no magazine in it. Sliding his hand down into the gun, he grasped the restrainer with his sweaty hand and pulled. It didn't move.

"Come on, come on..." Roy chanted to himself, feeling the slick metal slice through his skin on his hand. The weapon became slippery with blood.

The ships were finalizing their cross. Before long, they would be too far away for the cell to even hit them. With the last remainder of his strength, multiplied by fear, he gave a final tug and snapped the restrainer off of the gun. He let it drop through the ship. The blast chamber was open.

He jammed the pistol blast into the chamber and slammed the contraption shut. *Crude and short range, but it should work.* He raised the weapon to his shoulder and aimed it at the broken bolt. *With any luck, this should do enough damage to the emergency system to trigger it,* Roy thought, and without hesitation, pulled the trigger. The gun kicked abnormally, and it clattered from his hands and down to the decks below. But, the damage had been done. The emergency system clicked and whirred as broken cogs slammed up against each other. The releases snapped instantaneously, and in the blink of an eye, the cell catapulted out of its holding area. The release doors were still closed, but that didn't stop it. The cell smashed open the hatch and rocketed through the clouds like a missile.

The ships had no time to alter course. The cell blasted through the hull armor of the larger ship like it was paper, and it disappeared from view. Only a second later, it collided through decks, walls and doors to the fuel storage. It ruptured their cells almost instantly. A great explosion rang through Roy's ears as the larger ship burst into flames. Crewmen emerged onto the deck, on fire and their skin boiling. Many threw themselves overboard through the clouds rather suffer through the last seconds of their life. The flames licked the ship's balloon, and down it went, spiraling through the sky as the deck collapsed into itself. Only burning timbers remained.

The smaller of the ships, however, was a different story. It took a hit from the shockwave, and then spun out of control - but they were intact. The bow of their ship was aimed directly at the *Exodus*, and they were accelerating with no way to alter course.

THE EXODUS PROJECT

CHAPTER FIVE

CRASH LANDING

They had mere seconds. Smoke filled Roy's vision; the *Exodus* was on fire again. He was coughing, and his vision was tunneling. The ship was lurching violently and he couldn't stand. The pirate ship loomed closer, both of its engines destroyed in the explosion. Every couple of seconds, a desperate blast would be fired from somewhere aboard the *Exodus*, but it had little effect. Nothing could be done.

Wooden beams crashed down around him as the bow of the pirate ship connected with their hull. Both of their hulls fractured and splintered, the long, rounded bow of the pirate ship driving deep into the *Exodus*, not far from Roy's location. The pirate's balloon was shredded, and they were dropping much faster than the *Exodus*. This extra speed gradually began to slide the ship free of the wound, and finally, it fell below them. The threat was gone, but now they had other problems. The ship began to tilt dangerously towards the side that the cell was loosed from. Roy had to cling to the guardrail to avoid falling, as the ship was almost diagonal.

Roy pulled himself over towards the communications grid, but of course, it was heavily damaged, along with several other systems. It was a fragile device and couldn't even function in a disruption signal, let alone a ship - to - ship collision.

"What did you DO?!" said a shocked doctor Fitzroy, accompanied by Ferren, whose assessment of the situation was much less panicked, as they entered the deck. Ferren clutched a small manual in his hands, leafing through it and running his hands through his hair. He was mumbling to himself.

"Oooh..." He was moaning, but not in agony. "We are breaking so many protocols..."

"The ship is incredibly off - balanced, thanks to you," the doctor said with an eye roll. For an older man, he was surprisingly irritating.

"Protocol sixty - eight," Ferren kept mumbling. "Never engage in open combat. Protocol forty..."

"I know, I know." Roy pulled the doctor along as he made his way across the deck. Ferren followed, but almost sub - consciously, continuing to ramble. "The automatic backup was destroyed in the impact," Roy explained quickly as they approached the far side of the deck. "We'll need to disengage another cell."

"Protocol eighty - one, never engage to destroy. Protocol sixteen, never come into direct hull-to-hull impact with unknown ships."

"Help me with the manual controls!" Roy commanded, and the doctor came to his side. In intense situations, he could be very serious, but his personality still flourished. The ship gave a jolt and leaned even further to the side. The port engine began to cough and sputter.

"We don't have much time!" the doctor said as he opened the hatch to the manual controls. The area around the ship began to come into view again as they dropped out of the dust - colored clouds.

"Protocol one hundred and eighty-four, never drop below cloud level while hostiles remain two kilometers from the manned ship."

Together, the doctor and Roy pried the hatch open. Sure enough, on the inside, the controls were labeled *emergencies only* in bold, blood red letters. They were simple enough; a single, fist - sized button encased in thin glass. A tiny mallet was set to the side of it.

"Protocol six, never disengage steam cells mid-flight. Oh, but look, you broke that one already." The thin glass broke under the weight of the mallet. "Protocol thirty-nine, always keep sharp and dangerous objects away from steam cells."

Lester Fitzroy and Roy gave each other a nod before they smashed the button down with their palms. A warning alarm barely had time to go off before the cell's restraints loosened much quicker than design parameters specified. The massive object was torn violently from its resting place in the clamps and launched from the ship. The emergency doors hadn't been opened yet, but they didn't stand in its way. Although it only seemed to consist of steam and thick cloth, it was actually reinforced with heavy metal alloys and supports. The small emergency hatch was blasted to splinters as the cell was carried off by the wind. It quickly disappeared from sight, and the effects took hold within seconds. The ship was stabilizing.

"Protocol seventy-nine, ensure emergency hatches are open before attempting a manual cell release-"

"Oh, will you SHUT UP!" The doctor flared, spinning on his heel and backhanding the manual from Ferren's grasp. It fluttered over the edge and was gone. The doctor's coat billowed around him, adding to his threatening stance. Ferren said nothing, as he watched his principles by which he lived by fall through the sky. Roy watched it too, but for what reason he did not know. It was irrelevant, as Ferren would have concluded.

"Oh no..." Ferren moaned as he leaned over the rail of the ship. Roy followed his gaze, and they gasped.

"You can't honestly be grieving over the loss of your precious manual!" The doctor snapped, but that wasn't what they were looking at. Ferren and Roy beckoned him over and they looked down.

Below them wasn't the unforgiving blue salt water that they all feared was their fate. It was green. An island. His fear of heights began to take hold, portraying the many ways he could die by falling from such a height. *The rail could break, weakened by the battle. He might not even survive the crash land. Even - Stupid thoughts.*

"Why is it green?" Ferren inquired in awe. "Sand isn't green!"

"You've seen too much of home, lad," the doctor said, clapping him on the shoulder, oddly compassionate. Despite his calm gesture, Roy could tell by the look on his face that he was tense. "That's grass."

The ship was continuing to stabilize. They no longer had to hold to the rails to keep from falling. It was almost level. As the three looked down, they heard the mass broadcast alarm sound. The captain was smart. Even if ship communication was lost, he could use the broadcast system to get a message around. "All hands, this is the captain!" The second statement was rather irrelevant, as every member of the crew was familiar with the captain's booming voice. "Secure your stations! We are going to attempt an emergency landing!"

A second, fainter voice came over the broadcast. "We're gonna die!" It wailed in fear. Obviously, the bridge crew lacked a certain confidence.

"Well?" the doctor said after a moment of hesitation. "You heard the man! Secure your station!"

Ferren and Roy rushed to the closed-off area of the deck. The doctor quickly joined them when he realized returning to the medical bay probably wasn't an option, and they tied down everything that wasn't nailed there in the first place. Old modules and spare parts, bits and pieces remaining from the hull modifications and just old junk in general strewn about. *It was strange. Being Ferren's station, he kept it quite untidy, while the room he and Roy shared was always sparkling clean.*

The deck had begun to shake. A few of the bindings they had put around the loose objects shook free. The trio quickly re-tied them. One of the spare objects about the room, an altimeter, had found its way into Ferren's hands. He was constantly checking it.

"Were going down way too fast!" he reported. The doctor opened his mouth to reply with a sarcastic remark when Roy intervened.

"I read somewhere that in the event of a crash landing of any kind, it's safer to stay under something solid!" Roy gestured to the desk in the corner of the untidy room. He and Ferren crammed under it, but there was no room for the doctor. He insisted they use it for cover instead of him, reciting along with it a medical oath;

"If it comes between your life or the life of a patient, the patient shall live."

"Roughly composed, but it will suffice," Ferren remarked. Roy envied him at times to remain so calm in the face of imminent destruction. Roy's eyes were glued to the altimeter decide in Ferren's hands. *Two thousand feet... Nineteen hundred... Eighteen hundred...*

Roy held his breath and made the sign of the cross. He noticed the doctor do the same.

Twelve hundred... Eleven hundred...

They were at a thousand feet and dropping. Without warning, a sense of serenity overcame Roy. He fearlessly opened his eyes and looked around. He wondered if this was the calm that so many literary writers described as the feeling before death. The sounds of the world became distorted as if hearing it from underwater.

Roy wasn't looking at their altitude as it dropped below one hundred. There was an explosive crash, a sharp pain exploded behind his eyes, and everything went black.

Chapter Six

Stranded

The first thing Roy realized when he opened his eyes was that he was alive. Slowly, his senses began to come back to him - touch, smell, taste. He was lying on a cold, wooden floor, but on which deck, he did not know. He tried to stand, but his body responded with a stabbing pain down his leg. He wouldn't be able to go anywhere without medical assistance.

The *Exodus* didn't look like it was in very good shape. Broken glass and smashed beams lay strewn about the room, which, judging by the tipped tables and broken chairs, must have been the mess hall. Somehow, he had been thrown from the cargo bay all the way to the mess hall. *No wonder I ache so much.*

"Oww..." A recognizable voice moaned nearby. Roy looked around to find a crumpled heap of black cloth and red curls a few yards from his position. Only one member of the Exodus crew would dress like that, and of course, it was Emily the stewardess.

He was obviously in the mess hall. Using his better leg, he dragged himself over to her. For whatever reason, his mind took that moment to realize how attractive she actually was, with her round, dimpled cheeks and soft brown eyes that looked too big for her head-

Stupid thoughts.

Setting his feelings aside for another time, Roy shook her shoulder gently. She groaned a bit but raised her head to see who rudely awakened her from her nap. A gash in her forehead was bleeding something fierce, running around the corners of her mouth and pooling on the wooden deck. She gave a weak smile. "Hey, sugar..." she murmured, not breaking tradition with her nicknames. "We got creamed, huh?"

"Pretty much." Roy helped her to her feet, despite barely being able to stand himself. "We should find the doctor. He can patch us up." Emily could do little more than nod weakly in agreement. After a moment's hesitation, Roy slid his arm around her shoulder to support her. She did the same, and together, they limped from the mess hall.

Roy had never really considered relationships with girls. Since only men were permitted into the flight academy, he had always assumed he would be living out his days as a confirmed bachelor. Pursuing other relationships seemed out of the question.

Thankfully, the doctor's temporary residence was on the same deck as the mess hall, just two sections down. With luck, that would be the first place the doctor would go in a situation like this. But a sudden fear crept into Roy's mind - *what if Emily didn't make it that far?* The entire white ribbon and front of her dress was stained a deep scarlet, and they were practically leaving a trail of blood spots where they walked. Emily began to hang on his shoulder more and more the farther down the deck they went. Roy picked up the pace as gently as possible.

They passed section B of the deck and were now in section C. The sickbay was supposed to be set up here. Despite having never been there before, Roy was able to locate it. A crude red cross had been painted on the door, obviously without the captain's permission, and it was slightly ajar. With his free hand, Roy pulled it open.

Sure enough, there stood Doctor Lester Fitzroy. He was currently in the process of trying to stand a fallen medical bed back to its original position. He turned when he heard the door open and dropped the bed at the sight of the bleeding stewardess, and his doctor mode switched on.

"Get me a bandage!" he barked to Roy as he took his place by Emily's side and directed her towards one of the few standing beds. Roy limped off to a fallen pile of equipment and found a bandage roll. He quickly returned to the doctor.

"Easy..." He was murmuring as he helped Emily onto the bed. It was already beginning to stain itself red. The doctor snatched the bandaging out of Roy's outstretched palm and, with the speed and skill of a surgeon, wrapped a large section if it around Emily's forehead. The first few layers he applied were instantly soaked through with blood, but after applying several more, the bleeding began to slow. The doctor wrapped it around a couple more times just to be sure, and then sighed in relief.

"She's going to be fine." he said to Roy.

"Her eyes are shut," Roy said. "Is she-"

"She's just unconscious. She lost a lot of blood and will probably need several weeks to recover. Besides, head wounds bleed a lot." the doctor assured him. "But, in the meantime, you don't look too good either."

The doctor diagnosed Roy with serious bruising around his right calf and a minor concussion. "It's a miracle you didn't break it." Doctor Fitzroy murmured in his usual melancholy tone. "You should be able to walk fine. Try not to put too much pressure on it for the next few days, if at all possible," he added, with a slight eye roll.

"Understood." Roy stood from the bed and found an emergency medical kit among the debris, slightly dented but still containing its usual compliment of supplies.

"Where do you think you're going with that?" the doctor said suddenly, dropping his current task to stride over to Roy. "I might need that, and you're in no condition to be prancing around the ship!"

"I know where I'm going, doctor," Roy reassured him and made for the door. "The captain could need me."

"Oh, drop the heroic antics, will you!" The doctor spat so viciously that it made Roy flinch. "It's a miracle you're alive now with as few injuries as you have! You've been lucky so far, I'll admit that, but it's bound to run out eventually, so don't come crying to me when it does." Roy had been lucky. He had to admit that much. But in a split second he made his decision. Shouldering the oddly weighted medical kit, he left the sickbay.

Roy was going up. Before, as he had made his way down the corridor, he hadn't noticed the awkward angle at which the Exodus rested. He had to lean heavier and heavier on the wall as he went to prevent himself from falling over. He winced at the thought of how much damage the Exodus took during that encounter, including casualties.

The advantage of having an angle to rest on meant climbing the rigging was like walking on a slowly inclining hill. He was able to crawl up it with ease like some sort of jungle animal, despite his leg. He passed three decks and was almost to the bridge - his intended destination - until he stopped to look around. He had cleared the treetops and was able to fully grasp the size and complexion of this island. The first and most notable point of interest was its color. Roy had never seen so many shades of green in a single sight before in his life. It seemed as if each tree had its own specific shade, unlike any other. But the trees were what truly took him aback. *They were massive, towering structures, and there were so many of them. Back in my hometown, trees were considered a luxury to see fully grown, but I had always been told that trees grew to be a few feet tall, at most. These ones rivaled the height of the Exodus herself.*

Roy was easily able to see how they had come down, as they left a blackened gash through the trees. They had been lucky to have stopped when they did. A few hundred more meters and they would have been in the water. The ship itself came to a stop on the sandy shore on the eastern part of the island, tilted slightly in the direction of the sea.

After taking in the sights a little, Roy continued his climb. It wasn't long until his hands found the sharp edge of smashed glass lining the windowsill of the bridge. He pulled himself up and, carefully, over the sharp edges.

The bridge's conditions weren't good. The entire circular glass rim had been smashed to pieces, and senior staff members were strewn about the once organized room like discarded rag dolls. The navigation officer lay slumped across the small table littered with maps, near the far right of the room. A large shard of bloodstained glass at least a foot long protruded from his back. Roy didn't need a diagnosis from the doctor to come to the conclusion that he was dead.

Without warning, a figure leapt out from behind a pile of collapsed wooden beams, and Roy found himself staring down the barrel of a pistol. He instinctively closed his eyes, as if expecting the figure to fire, and stumbled over a bit of debris, dropping the medical kit. His mind raced. *Could one of the pirates have found a way aboard the Exodus*? He reached for his own pistol, but sure enough, he left it in the cargo bay what felt like eons ago. Eyes still closed, he awaited his inevitable end. But it didn't come. Slowly, he looked up.

"Captain?" he said in disbelief.

"Sorry to scare you," said Captain Arthur, extending his arm. Roy took it and pulled himself up. "I thought you might be one of them."

"No, sir." Roy murmured. "As far as I can tell, none of them made it on board."

"Good. They wouldn't be smart enough to board us with the few seconds they had to. Damn good thing, too. This gun doesn't fire anymore." The captain tossed it aside.

"Good to know." Roy couldn't help but to remark.

"Mmm." There was silence for a few seconds. Then, "How are the lower decks doing?"

"Not well. I got a look at them on my way up, but I'm not sure how severe the damage is."

"We should gather the remaining men. Figure out what we're going to do next."

"Agreed. Should we search for survivors deck by deck?"

"That would be best."

It took the two several hours to scour the ship for remaining crewmen. Soon, it became rather routine to Roy. From time to time he found someone. If they were wounded, he sent them to sickbay. If not, they helped him in his search. In the end, three hours later, his band of merry men emerged from the Exodus onto the sandy beach. He had thirty-eight with him and sent another twenty-two to sickbay. Fifty in total. Ferren wasn't among them.

It wasn't five minutes later that the captain emerged as well, with a couple dozen crew in tow. "Twenty-five," he reported. "Sixteen in sickbay."

"Is..." Roy waited until he was closer to the captain before continuing. "Is Ferren with you?"

The captain pursed his lips and shook his head. "That doesn't necessarily mean he's dead, Roy." If the captain had anything that could be considered a soft side, he was showing it now. "We still haven't searched the nooks and crannies of the Exodus yet. Don't lose hope."

Eighty-six. Eighty-six out of the two hundred fourteen survived, and only fifty of them were fit to do anything productive. Almost as a last resort, Arthur ordered a half dozen crewmen to search the catwalks and junctions between decks. A lot had happened and it was very possible some crewmen were holding out there. Roy decided to take the captain's advice and hope Ferren was among them, assuming they were even there.

But they very well couldn't be. Which meant Ferren wouldn't be with them. Stupid thoughts.

Roy shook his head and went to join a circle of crewmen, including one of the captain's senior officers. From the looks of him and the markings on his uniform, he was the communications operator.

"...Heard him talkin' to another crewman." He was saying to the younger cadets, who were all listening intently. "Said it 'imself. Said we're gonna die here, die of starvation. Said there ain't barely enough to feed his senior officers, that we'll be dead within a week."

He was obviously talking about the captain, and Roy immediately got defensive. "The captain said nothing of the sort," he said angrily, sitting among the cadets. "We're to keep morale up and spirits high, despite the situation we landed ourselves in."

"An' just who the 'ell are you?" The senior said, and he felt the eyes of the cadets sway to him as well. They weren't angry; they were just following his example.

"Roy. Roy Mulleary." he stood, attempting to hold a menacing form.

"Tanner," he stood as well. "Tanner Kassian."

The two stared each other down for quite a while, and Roy got a good look at him. He was a couple inches taller and probably had a good twenty pounds over him. He looked to be a year or two older, as well. Roy momentarily wondered how he rose to the rank of senior officer in just a year or two, but quickly pushed it away. Roy could already feel a dislike for this boy bubbling up inside him.

After quite a while of silence, the cadets quickly grew bored and left in search of something to do, leaving the two alone. As soon as the last cadet scurried off Roy hissed angrily at Tanner,

"Just why are you doing that?"

"Isn't it obvious?" He retaliated so quickly that he left Roy no time to recover. "We are going to die here, and we are going to run out of food. It's only a matter of time before a mutiny breaks out, and when it does, I want all the support I can get." A sly grin crept over his smug face.

"You... You..." Roy was at a loss for words. *He had the gall... The audacity to challenge the captain's judgment?* Tanner was the perfect example of a cocky cadet fresh from the academy, only in all the wrong ways. *A mutiny?!* Even Roy wouldn't think of doing that, despite being a bit of a rule breaker himself.

Tanner smirked and poked at the sand with a long stick. "We are going to die out here, Roy Mulleary. Captain or no captain."

CHAPTER SEVEN
PERFECT RECALL

Probably for the best, the captain called a meeting for the remainder of the crew. It wasn't much. The tally had risen to ninety - two after the captain's last search - Ferren, however, was still not among the survivors.

Captain Arthur spoke. "I will admit," he began. "That this is far from a preferable situation. Seemingly stranded, our own Exodus crippled beyond repair. And even if we could fix her, we lack the steam to get her lifted. Hopeless?" A bit surprised by the captain's melancholy remarks, many of the transfixed crewmen nodded and even agreed. The captain grew stern.

"NO!" he burst in anger when they agreed. "Absolutely not! Communications reported getting a distress call out just before we crashed. Things may look grim now, but look on the bright side!"

The silence of the crew was unnaturally loud.

"We're going to be distributing weapons shortly," the captain said, ending his attempted motivational speech. "Unfortunately, not enough rifles were recovered for everyone to have one. Whether you receive one or not, you are welcome to use any debris you can find to fashion a weapon of your own. Understood?"

The crew responded less than optimistically. The captain was never much of a speaker, let alone a motivational one. It probably took him all morning to piece together his attempted speech. It was a shame he didn't get any further, for it was a grand start. Not all that unique, but it was to be expected from the experienced captain.

Not long after the meeting, some of the remaining tactical crewmen set up a makeshift armory alongside the helpless Exodus. Unfortunately, they allotted the remaining rifles on a first come first served basis, and by the time Roy arrived at the front, they had little more to give him than the sand beneath their boots. Rather disheartened, Roy went out to find a makeshift weapon.

As he made his way to one of the larger debris fields, Roy noticed Tanner gallivanting about some of the newer recruits with a shiny, brass barreled rifle clutched in his hands. Roy's dislike for the overconfident bastard only increased.

About an hour later, or so he thought; few working clocks were salvaged, with bloody fingertips and scarred palms, Roy recovered a moderately-sized, blade - shaped slice of metal from the pile, most likely from an engine propeller. It was about a foot and a half long, the perfect size to work as a close-range machete. Using some old leather straps once used as rigging, he wrapped a handle for the thing. As he swung it experimentally through the air, however, he winced. It was weighted awkwardly, the handle was loose and uncomfortable, and the edge was dull and bent from the impact. In is frustration, he gave the thing another violent chop to his left.

"Hey!" A voice shrieked, and for a moment of fear, Roy thought that he had just ended someone's existence. But a quick check revealed no blood on his crude machete, and Ferren standing beside him.

Ferren?

A well of emotion sprung up within Roy. For a moment, his feelings of fear, confusion, surprise, shock, and disbelief collided within him and he stood rooted to the spot, unable to speak. Ferren's face remained unchanged, as usual.

"Yes?" he said after the long pause.

Roy only had one thing to say. "You're alive?"

Ferren's eyebrow went up. "Of course."

"But you... You weren't found in the wreckage!"

"That's because I wasn't in the wreckage," he remarked in his usual, emotionless voice. "I woke up about a couple hour walk that way." He gestured with his hand to the dense sea of trees."

"And you made it-" Roy began to ask, but he was done with questions. Instead, he just laughed. "You will never cease to amaze me, my friend," he said, clapping a hand on Ferren's shoulder.

"But you," Something that could actually be considered a smile crept across Ferren's face. "Need to watch where you swing that thing." He gestured to Roy's machete, and they both shared a laugh. For a moment there, it felt like everything was fine - they were back on the Exodus, having a coffee at four in the morning and sharing their stories of difficult childhoods. But, of course, they were stranded, on an island, in the middle of nowhere, with a wrecked ship and a handful of first-year cadets who barely knew how to tie their shoes.

Roy was loving life.

Ferren helped Roy stabilize his homemade weapon, but it wasn't by much - the thing was still hellish to hold, and even worse to use. As they worked together, Roy filled him in on the few events that he missed - including his meeting with Tanner.

"I just don't understand him," Roy remarked as they re-wrapped the handle. "Usually, that spirit of rebellion and, yes, even mutiny, dies out within a year. This one's obviously been doing this for years, with little change of heart."

"Some simply don't mature," Ferren replied almost instantaneously like it was the most obvious thing in the world. "Like you said, that spirit usually dies off - but everyone has a different background. If he enjoys attention, he will want to do things ridiculous or uncalled for in by our standards. But for him, he could just be trying to survive in the only way he sees fit - having allies."

Roy thought this over. "I still don't like the bastard." He spat bitterly, despite being surprisingly understanding of Tanner's position.

"Give this a try." Ferren handed Roy the refitted machete. Roy gave it an experimental swing and saw little improvement. Still, he thanked Ferren for his assistance.

"How are the others holding up?" Ferren asked after a while of silence.

"You can ask them yourselves." Roy gestured towards the sandy edge of the island where most of the crew wandered aimlessly. The two of them returned to the group together.

Captain Arthur had found two more survivors within the wreckage, bringing them up to ninety - four. That tally quickly increased to ninety - five with the appearance of Ferren. When he saw the two, he beckoned them over.

"I'm going to be sending out search teams in groups of three," Arthur said. "One every hour, and we'll rotate until nightfall. We're starting to get the feeling that we aren't alone here."

"And we will be going with a search team?" Roy jumped to the point.

"Yes, you will," the captain replied flatly. "Your team's next, in about a half hour or so. Bring a cadet along."

"Yes, sir," Roy and Ferren said simultaneously.

"Good, good..." the captain said awkwardly, before turning and walking over to Doctor Fitzroy. The captain was never a very outspoken person, even in his younger years. And he had, most likely, never been in a scenario like this.

Roy and Ferren spent the next half hour searching amongst the remaining crew for a suitable cadet. Eventually, they found a short, sharp - eyed first year who stood out from the depressing mood of the rest of the crew. They found him sprawled out on the beach with his hands crossed behind his head and gazing up at the clouds. The huge puddle's water - which, as Roy recalled from the academy, was known as the *ocean* - lapped up onto the sand just below his feet. The one thing that set him apart was that he looked relaxed. He introduced himself.

"It's Charlie," the boy said, shaking both Roy's and Ferren's hands with a firm grip. He had a strange accent. He pronounced his *a*'s and *o*'s as in *aw* and never actually finished a lot of his words, as if the ending was understood.

"So, Charlie," Roy began, sitting beside him. "Have you considered our offer?"

"I have, and my answer is *sure as hell yes*" Charlie pushed himself to his feet, and Roy joined him. "I've been bored out of my bloody mind here, and a chance for some action pops up? The only thing that needs considering, mate," he jabbed a finger at Roy and Ferren. "Is your considering it done."

"Good." Roy shook hands with him again. He was a likable boy, and surprisingly mature for only being a first year.

"I think it's almost on the hour," Ferren said, squinting up at the sky. "We should be getting back to the captain soon."

"Yeah, we have about seven minutes or so," Charlie said almost without hesitation.

Roy blinked. "Do you have a clock?"

Charlie shrugged. "No, but see the sun now? When it was there yesterday, the time was about seven minutes to the hour."

Roy's confidence in the boy's maturity was fading fast. "It could be off by any few inches from what you remember," Roy attempted to explain. "It just... can't be in the exact same place as before."

"Oh, no," Charlie shook his head. "You don't understand. It's my memory. I was born with perfect recall."

Ferren lit up like a Christmas tree. "Really?" he practically squeaked. "I've never met one before! Is it true you actually remember the exact amount of heartbeats you've had in a lifetime? How many steps have you taken in this last year? Do you actually have to -"

"Ferren," Roy said, placing a hand on his shoulder. "Not now."

Ferren opened his mouth to speak again, but thought better of it and shut it. "Sorry," he murmured.

"Right," Charlie said, a bit hesitantly. "Let's be going, shall we?"

"Right," the two said in reply. Roy could already begin to see the benefits of an associate with perfect recall. He could just imagine shutting up the irritating, egocentric members of the academy back home with the starting phrase, "As a matter of fact, I knew a guy..."

****

The new trio wasted no time in reporting to the captain before gathering some supplies, including emergency rations, water, and a radio, and setting off. Roy was surprised at how thin the forest of trees was. The initial barrier between the beach and forest was heavily dense, but after a few minutes of walking, the only thing that barred their path was the occasional boulder or small cluster of trees.

"So," Ferren said as he jogged to catch up with Charlie. "Ah, about my questions about perfect recall..."

"Yes, yes," Charlie replied as they walked. "You asked if we can really remember how many heartbeats we've experienced and if we can count our steps subconsciously?"

All Ferren could do was nod, eagerly awaiting an answer. Roy could already see that Ferren found Charlie to be almost a God-like figure, with skills and traits he did not currently possess. People can be dangerous with these kinds of idols; not necessarily to the people around them, but to themselves.

"You see, mate," Charlie began, as Ferren listened intently; "Perfect recall doesn't mean that you indefinitely remember every tiny detail about everything you've ever done. It just means that you can retain information for longer periods of time and that it is more easily recalled when a similar sense is experienced, be it sound, smell, taste, touch, etcetera."

Ferren dimmed a little. "So... you don't actually remember how many heartbeats you've experienced?"

Charlie chuckled. "No. No, I don't."

"Ah." Ferren backed off a bit before dropping behind to talk to Roy. "Well, that was..." He began.

"Depressing?" Roy suggested.

"That would just about sum it up." said Ferren.

"Life is full of disappointments."

"So I have been learning." The two shared a lighthearted laugh. It felt good to laugh sometimes.

Roy had to stop himself and Ferren in their tracks to avoid from colliding with Charlie. He had stopped, without warning and was staring off into the distance as if in a trance.

"Something wrong?"

"No, no..." Charlie murmured squinting off into the distance. "D'ya see that? Over there?"

"What?" Roy asked, following his gaze. "I can't see anything."

"Nor I." Ferren chimed in.

"It's... Ugh, I don't know." Charlie shook his head. "I can't see it that well. Come on, let's get a closer look."

Ferren raised his eyebrows. "Perfect recall and sharp vision... a truly groundbreaking ability."

Roy had to stifle a laugh. *Ferren was starting to understand sarcasm more and more as they progressed through the academy years.* The two ran to catch up with Charlie.

"You really didn't see it?" he asked as the two caught up.

"What's *it*?" Roy pressed, ignoring the question.

"I don't bloody know!" Charlie retaliated. "But *it's* massive and grey, whatever it is."

They picked up the pace from there on out as they went down a small valley. The base of the first hill was wet and humid, like a swamp. Their boots were soaked by the time they reached and began to climb the next hill.

Roy reached the top first and helped Ferren and Charlie up. He noticed that Charlie as probably the stronger of the three, which could prove to be beneficial.

"Thanks, mate," Charlie said as he pulled himself over the lip of the valley. "Jeez, my boots are gonna be soaked for-" He stopped.

"Charlie?" Roy called over his shoulder as he pulled Ferren up. "Charlie?" He got no response. As soon as Ferren was on his own two legs, he turned around. "Oh." Was all he could say. "Oh... My."

"*Oh my's* friggin right," Charlie said back, without peeling his eyes from the spectacle before them.

It was a while before anyone spoke. "Y'know, the more I think about it," Roy eventually began. "'Massive and grey' isn't that bad of a description." Just over the valley, hidden beneath the umbrella of trees, was a huge, grey, stone fortress.

Chapter Eight

Discovery

"This could be decades old," Roy breathed as he ran his hand over the broken-down, decaying wall of the fortress.

"I'm thinking more like centuries," Charlie countered in an equally awed tone of voice. "Do you see a way in?"

"I think there's a door around here," Ferren called from around the first wall of the fortress. The other two followed him around until they came to a huge set of wooden doors, reinforced with thick metals. A huge set of brass door knockers hangs from each side, as big around as a watermelon. Roy approached one and, grasping it firmly, pulled it up and let it fall. A resounding boom echoed through the decaying fortress.

"Just in case anyone's in there," Charlie remarked. "Y'know, wouldn't want to disturb them."

"Right." Roy wasn't listening. "Come help me open this," he commanded, and the other two took their places next to him. "On three."

"Oh, just push." Charlie eagerly snapped, and the trio heaved, digging their heels into the softened soil. The door creaked and groaned, but the metal enforced wood held firmly.

"This isn't going to move," Ferren said when they stopped. "Look. The hinges have rusted right through to the reinforced edge. We wouldn't get this thing open with a battering ram."

"If the hinges are such a problem," Charlie said, drawing his pistol. "Can't we just shoot them off?"

"I wouldn't," Ferren advised, placing a hand on the weapon's slide. "See the archway above the door?" he pointed. Sure enough, it was missing the main keystone holding it up. "We could bring the entire thing down, and I wouldn't want to be under it when that happened."

"Alright." Charlie holstered the weapon. "So, how are we going to get in?"

Roy looked around. "There," he finally said, pointing to a lower section of the wall. "I might be able to climb that."

"I don't know, mate," Charlie warned. "That's a long way down from the top."

"I'll take my chances," Roy assured him as he made his way to the wall. He could faintly hear Doctor Fizroy's words echoing through his head. "You've been lucky so far, I'll admit that, but it's bound to run out eventually, so don't come crying to me when it does." Roy didn't realize how right the doctor might be.

He came to the weakened section of wall and tested the handholds. At least the ones he could reach from the ground seemed sturdy enough, but anything could be said for the ones higher up. Roy rubbed his hands together and began his climb. The first half held relatively well, probably due to the fact that it had the support of the upper wall, pushing down on it. But the higher up he got, the looser the wall became. As he reached for a higher handhold, the stone Roy's foot rested on came loose, and fell. He scrambled and, luckily, was able to lodge his foot in the hole the falling stone made.

"Careful!" Ferren and Charlie said, almost simultaneously.

"I know!" Roy returned, not exactly in the mood for conversation. Wordlessly, he continued his climb until he neared the top. By now, the stones were completely loose, so Roy was able to push them off until he could find a more stable one to vault over. When he was no longer able to push them off, he took hold of the highest point and swung his feet over. As soon as his feet cleared the wall, the section he was holding on to crumbled, and he found himself clinging to dust. Before he could even let out a scream, he was tumbling through the air towards certain death.

What a way to go, he thought. *The doctor was right.* Then moments later, *What am I thinking? The doctor was most certainly not ri-*

Roy's internal argument was suddenly halted when he came to a stop rather early. He could hear the groan of wood planks and smelled the faint smell of sawdust. Pain was registering in his shoulder. Gradually, he opened his eyes. He had landed on some kind of elevated wooden platform conveniently located about halfway down the backside of the wall. He reluctantly pushed himself up. The platform was shaky, and he stood slowly. From here, he would easily be able to climb back down the rest of the wall. "Thank you conveniently placed platform." Roy murmured and took a step forward.

Little did he know, the third leg of the platform had been completely rotten through, and Roy's weight had almost broken it. However, with the sudden change of pressure, the leg snapped like a bent knee, and along with it went the other three. This time, Roy had a chance to scream before crashing down to the solid, stone floor. Pain rocketed down his spine and through his arms and legs. He laid there among the broken planks of wood for quite some time before returning to reality.

"Oh God..." he murmured. "Oh God, that hurt."

"Hey!" Roy heard Charlie's muffled voice from behind the door. "What the hell are you doing?"

"Sorry!" Roy called back, his voice cracking. "Just... taking my time, is all."

"Well, hurry up!"

"Yeah, yeah... gimme a second, I'll have the door open." Roy managed to push himself up to his feet despite the flaming response from his lower back. He limped over to the backside of the door, where he not only noticed further rusting of the hinges but also a thick wooden beam that had been lowered across the entrance being held in place by metal shelves secured to the wall. It was several inches thick, and in surprisingly good condition for possibly having been decades, or even hundreds of years old. He braced his shoulder under it and pushed it over the shelves. It fell aside.

"Alright," he called over the wall. "You should be able to open it now."

He heard the grunts and groans of Ferren and Charlie from beyond the wall. Slowly, the hinges began to snap and shear, before having been pried open enough for them to slip through.

"Are you hurt?" Ferren asked Roy as soon as he was inside.

"I don't think any damage was done," Roy replied as lightheartedly as possible. "I was lucky that platform was there."

"I think it was more of a scaffolding." Ferren corrected. "I also think that this was an unfinished structure, which would explain the construction scaffolding and unfinished wall."

"Indeed," Roy wasn't really listening, but he got the basic idea. When around over-analytical people like Ferren, it was a skill that had to be learned or friendship would never last. "Should we take a look around?"

"Probably," Ferren absorbed the surroundings of the inside of the fort for a moment, and so did Roy. It seemed a lot smaller on the inside than it had looked on the outside. They were standing in an entryway, which lead to a series of rooms and eventually a small, mossy courtyard. It was obviously made without style or comfort in mind, but instead, order and easy access, allowing for little breathing room.

"A cramped little place," Charlie remarked.

"There," Ferren pointed to one of the rooms. "That would probably be their equivalent of a command center."

"Let's check it out." Roy and the others stepped through the entryway and ducked through the door to the supposed control center. There were small tables surrounding the room, scattered with materials and parchments, and a scarlet and navy blue banner hung above the doorway.

"No way." Roy blurted. The other two turned and saw the banner as well.

"Uh oh," was all Charlie could say. All three of them were easily able to recognize the moody colors of the pirates.

"Are they here?" Ferren asked, mostly to himself. "How could they be here?"

But the more they examined the banner, the more obvious it became. "No..." Roy approached the markings. "No, this isn't right. Look, this banner is as old as this fortress," he ran the banner through his fingers, and sure enough, it was easily pulled apart by the strings. "Whoever put this here wasn't them. Or at least, not the ones who attacked us."

"While that is comforting, don't get me wrong," Charlie insisted. "But why is it here? I mean, all the way out here? Even away from the drought, the famine... why?"

"I'm not sure," Roy started towards the tables around the room. "But I get the idea these can help us figure it out."

"Good idea." Ferren started at one end of the tables while Roy began towards the other. Charlie was attempting to remove the banner without it disintegrating.

Roy's table was littered with parchments with ancient writing on its surface. Upon closer examination, he realized it was written in Latin.

"Ferren, come here," without taking his eyes off the parchment, Roy beckoned him over. "How's your late, fifth century Latin?"

"A bit rusty," Ferren admitted. "But doable. Found some?"

"Yeah. Quite a bit." For once, Roy regretted having slept through his eight semesters of ancient Latin. Ferren came beside him over and shuffled through the parchment.

"Well, it's... sort of Latin," Ferren murmured, almost to himself. "Very late, though; towards when the language broke apart."

"Can you read it?"

"Most of it," he admitted and continued shuffling through the papers. "Here. This looks important," he pulled out something that looked like a formal letter.

"What's it say?" Charlie appeared over their shoulders, with the falling apart banner in his hands.

"It's a letter," Ferren began.

"Oh, that's bloody useful." Charlie murmured.

"Hey," Roy waved a hand at him. "Let him finish."

"Looks like it was to a certain... Baker Lee," Ferren concluded. "From a William Iliad. Strange names."

"Strange indeed," Charlie remarked. "So, what's our friend Will have to say?"

"William," Ferren corrected, then read what he could. "Let's see... 'My acquaintance master Baker, it is with satisfaction that I am...' Endorsing? What the hell? Oh, no, writing. It's writing. 'Writing to you this day to send word that the construction of our outpost has been a great success. We expect to be finished within a week. It would be an earlier date, but the ground below one of the walls contains a tunnel, and we are having difficulty making it stand. Even so, it should not prove to be a problem for much longer. Signed William Baker, quartermaster of the...'"

Ferren stopped. "Huh," he murmured. "That's strange."

"What?" Charlie and Roy chimed simultaneously.

"The word here, it's... 'Prophets', but it's written like a proper noun."

"Prophets?" Charlie asked. "Could that be the name of their... Order... or organization maybe?"

"It's very possible," Ferren concluded. "But that's a pretty high and mighty name for some rowdy pirates, don't you think? Especially the language used here... too formal for them."

"Could these people just be..." Roy was thinking, not listening. "That same Order?"

"I think the condition of this fortress can denounce that hypothesis." Ferren retorted.

"It can down here," Roy leaned forward on the table. "But not up there," he pointed up.

"You think they continued their legacy with airships?" Ferren caught on. "And it fell apart until they became what they are today?"

"Exactly." Roy's eyes glinted with a sense of discovery.

"But that still doesn't explain why they're all the way out here." Charlie crossed his arms across his chest. "I mean, this is possibly the most insignificant place to build an outpost."

"Maybe that was the point," Roy predicted. "They could have been a kind of underground organization."

"All we can do at this point is guess," Ferren said, ending the debate. "But, for now, this isn't important. Let's look around, see if we can find any useful supplies."

"Right." They continued into the next room through a wooden door. The first thing they noticed was the unforgiving odor.

"Ugh, who died in here?" Charlie blurted, pulling his shirt up over his nose.

"I think this was a food storage," Ferren said, also pulling his short over his nose. "That would explain the odor."

"And the flies," Roy added.

"Even so, it might not have all gone bad," Ferren stepped toward the origin of the scent, a locked door. "Charlie, can you shoot the lock off?"

Charlie took a glance at the lock. "The whole thing's rusted. It should come off easily." He drew his weapon. "Stand back."

The others complied as Charlie took aim and pulled the trigger. A bang went off, and the lock crumbled and fell to the floor.

"Good shot," Roy said as he stepped toward the door, pressing his collar tighter over his face. "Hold your breaths." He reached forward and pushed the door open.

"Christ!" Charlie exclaimed, stepping back. Not only had the odor amplified, but it wasn't food that was in that door.

It was bodies.

"Ew." Ferren murmured, staring at the pile of corpses. "They look like they were attacked."

"And the bodies hidden in here," Roy finished. "Grisly."

"Indeed." Without hesitation, he shut the door. "Let's leave them at peace."

"No argument here," Charlie remarked as they quickly exited the room.

"So, what now?" Roy leaned up against one of the tables with the parchment. "Do we leave now?"

"I was thinking we could-" Ferren suddenly stopped, and cocked his head to the side, as if listening.

"What?" Charlie said and got no response from Ferren. "Wha-"

"Shh!" Ferren waved a hand at him. "You hear that?"

"Hear wha-"

"Shh!"

They stopped and listened. At first, neither Roy nor Charlie heard anything. Then, voices. Faint ones.

"Is it one of our teams?" Roy whispered, but Ferren shook his head.

"No way," he insisted. "First, they're coming from the wrong direction, and second, they sound older. Much older than our cadets."

"So... Who are they?"

"I don't know, but I don't want to wait around to figure it out."

"Agreed." They all said. "Take everything you can carry from this room," Roy added, turning to the table. "Including that banner."

They loaded their bags and pockets with as much parchment and odds and ends from the room that they could hold. The voices were drawing closer, and from the bits and pieces of the things they were saying, it became clear that they were not Exodus crewmen.

"Look," Roy whispered, beckoning Ferren over. He held one of the parchment papers. "This isn't like the rest."

"You're right." Ferren studied it for a moment. "It looks like schematics of some sort, but I don't recognize it."

The voices were growing closer. Roy took the parchment and stuffed it away with the others, wincing as it tore in several places. They could begin to make out what was being said.

"...Boss says we'll take back anything of value," One was saying. "And kill on sight."

"I still can't believe they brought us down," another offered. "We had them outmanned and outgunned. And a measly cell, fired like a weapon? Between them and that doctor, I don't know which was worse."

Ferren and Roy's eyes locked. "It's them." They whispered at almost the same time.

"Entrance should be around here," the voice said. It was moving around the wall, approaching the doors.

"Back! Back!" Ferren whispered furiously, beckoning for the others to follow. They fled deeper into the fortress until they reached the courtyard. From there, there was no exit.

"I'm not going to be able to climb this," Roy warned then as they approached the back wall. "The only way out is the way we came back in."

"And through them?" Ferren squeaked.

"And through them," Roy confirmed. "We don't have much of a choice."

"Gotcha." Charlie and Ferren drew their pistols, and Roy unsheathed his crude weapon.

"I would advise against pistols for as long as you can," Roy cautioned. "One misfired shot and this whole place could come down. You saw how weak the walls were."

"Agreed," Ferren nodded to Charlie. "Take them out quietly."

They took a place at the doorway to the room with the tables, and pressing up, against the wall, they peeked around the corner. There were three of them, all armed with a kind of weapon none of them had seen before. It was almost like their own mercury rifles, only it lacked a stock of any kind and had a magazine almost three times as long. An odd, metal contraption was strapped to the ejection chamber.

"I would be careful of those," Ferren advised. "They look semi - automatic."

"Yeah, 'best weapons money can buy' my ass." Charlie looked disapprovingly at his own weapon.

"Ack! What is that smell?" one of the pirates exclaimed from the table room.

"Frankly, I don't care," another snapped. "And I don't want to know."

"Agreed. But hey, look. These have to be worth something." Of course, they meant the parchments left behind. Now they had incentive to stop them.

"Now," Roy mouthed and they moved up to the entrance to the room. "When one of them walks through, shoot the entryway's arch. It should knock it down. From there, we jump in and take them down hand-to-hand."

"That's pretty crude," Ferren couldn't help but remark, but he took aim at the archway anyway. "But doable."

"Right, let's go." Roy nodded to the others, then turned and struck his weapon across the stone. A resounding clang echoed through the place.

"What was that?" one of the pirates asked.

"Don't ask us! Go find out!" another snapped. The footsteps approached the door.

Roy waited a moment and then nodded to Ferren. He nodded back, and then pulled the trigger.

The blast crashed through the weak stone, practically disintegrating the keystone. The remaining supports crumbled down before knocking the pirate at the door to the ground, hard. He remained unmoving.

"There!" one if the pirates exclaimed, and raised his weapon. But Charlie was on him in a flash with his hands on the barrel, and the two began a struggle for the gun.

"Roy, get the other one!" Charlie called over his shoulder. Roy had no reason not to comply, so he rushed to the second pirate and drove his fist into his stomach with all his might. The man didn't budge. Slowly, Roy looked up to see the towering, seven and a half foot tall brute. He looked down at Roy like he was deciding how much fun he could have killing him. A grin crept across his face as he raised the weapon.

Roy ducked under his arm as blasts chewed into the floor where he stood, and using the wall as leverage, leapt up and drove his heels into the brute's elbow. Thankfully, it was just enough to weaken his grip on the weapon, and it clattered to the ground. Without hesitation, Roy kicked it under the door to the room with the bodies.

"I wouldn't go after that," Roy advised, and raised his fists and took three, hard swings, each connecting with the pirate's jawbone. Three satisfying cracks ran out in quick succession. Roy looked up, expecting to see his target in pain. He was most certainly not in pain. If anything, Roy just pissed him off.

Letting out a hideous bellow, the brute charged forward and tackled Roy and, almost scooping him up, drove him hard into the door leading to the courtyard. His head slammed against and splintered the wood while stars danced before his eyes, and his vision began to tunnel. "Ow..." he murmured and took a few more futile swings at the brute. Then, he remembered he had feet. Pulling his leg back, he shot it forward between the pirate's legs once, twice, three times. Even a man of his stature couldn't resist that, and he let Roy go, but not before the door crashed down, leaving them both sprawling in the overgrown grass of the courtyard.

"Oh..." Roy moaned, and for a moment of truce, they pushed themselves to their feet. "Come on, yeah?"

The pirate obviously accepted the challenge. He came at Roy like a freight train, and Roy was barely able to sidestep out of the way, delivering a few quick jabs to his attacker's head in the process. He still remained unharmed.

"Okay, punches don't work on you," Roy murmured to himself. "So what does?"

Again, the man charged, but as Roy sidestepped again, he changed direction and caught him around the waist, and with his massive arm, threw him into the stonework of the moss - covered fountain. Roy had no time to recover before he was grasped around the neck by strong hands and thrust head first into the murky fountain water.

Roy was surprisingly awed by the sensation of being underwater. Seeing as he was raised in a desert wasteland, the little water they could find was drunk right away, and from time-to-time, he would rinse himself with the water deemed unsafe to drink. He had always looked forward to those days.

Then, he remembered that he couldn't breathe. He began to kick and squirm, throwing punches at random. Few of them made contact. His head began to swim, and his chest burned. He tried to scream, but nothing but bubbles rose to the surface. He pushed in vain at the hands around his throat, but his strength was failing. He began to stop thinking, just focusing on the hands ending his existence. *It's over. I'm done.*

Just before he slipped out of consciousness, he heard a muffled poof from outside the water, then another. The hands around his neck slacked, and, gathering his remaining strength, he kicked the pirate away. His hands came loose and he surged upwards and broke the surface.

His vision was foggy, and Roy was pretty sure there was blood. Blood on the brute, blood on himself. Once he was able to see, he noticed the pirate standing over him. Roy flinched for a moment in fear of another of his devastating blows, but the man's arm fell to his side. He looked down. Blood was streaming down his chest and dripping to the overgrown grass. He looked up one last time, and then crumpled to the ground in the pooling blood.

Charlie and Ferren stood behind the brute, their weapons raised. Smoke gently rose from the end of their pistols. They lowered them and went to help Roy.

"You alright?" Charlie asked, extending his arm.

"Define 'alright'," Roy asked, taking Charlie's arm and pulling himself up.

"Some of them obviously survived the crash," Ferren offered as they made their way towards the entryway, Roy leaning heavily on Charlie. "They must have crashed here, too."

"Outmanned and outgunned," Roy murmured. "On a deserted island in the middle of nowhere."

"Yep," Charlie grunted. "Jeez, you're heavy."

Chapter Nine

Capture

Roy tossed their weapons down on the table before Captain Arthur. "They had these when they attacked us, sir," he explained. "That look like regularly single shot weapons, but were modified to be both semi-automatic and have a clip of fifteen shots."

The captain whistled. "And they told us we had the finest weaponry money can buy."

"Exactly-" Charlie began in an argumentative tone, but Ferren shushed him.

"Anyways, we have been able to confirm that at least one of the ships crashed here with us," Roy continued. "And that they know of our presence."

The captain was listening and stroking his beardless chin. "I see..." he murmured. "You've put me in a difficult position, you three have."

"Sir, I would recommend-"

"Quiet." The captain said in such a gentle tone that it took several seconds for Roy to register that he had even said it.

"Sir?"

"Sorry, but I'm thinking." The captain leaned against the table as if in pain for several seconds. "We'll need a defense perimeter around our site."

"Ferren and I can handle that." Charlie volunteered. "Anything else?"

"Not now, no." The captain said. "But, before any of you do more work, get some rest and something to eat. You haven't eaten since we crashed."

"With all due respect, sir, our comfort is of no concern-"

"Quiet," the captain repeated in his calm tone. "Get some rest. That's an order."

Roy opened his mouth to argue, but nothing came out. He couldn't argue, because he wanted nothing more than to sit back, relax, and eat some lamb chop flavored rations. Of course, it tasted nothing like lamb chops, but the label claiming it was, seemed good enough.

"Up for some lamb chops?" Roy put his arm around Ferren's shoulders and grinned.

"You mean cardboard?" Charlie added, and they laughed as they dug through one of the open crates of ration packs.

"One per person." A nearby cadet warned. He must have been at least a third year, and had a strong frame. None of them questioned him as they selected their own unique favors and then took a seat in the sand.

"Thanks, by the way," Roy said as they all crunched on their rations that were, indeed, quite similar to cardboard. "For the help, back there."

"Ah, don't mention it," Charlie said between mouthfuls. "Great chance for target practice."

"We didn't have much of a choice," Ferren added. "That man was a beast."

"Mmm." They ate in silence for a while.

"Oh, boy," Charlie murmured, nodding towards a group of cadets. "He's at it again."

Roy turned towards the cadets, and his optimism hit rock bottom. Tanner, irritating, annoying, egocentric Tanner was making his way through the cadets, clutching at least three ration packs.

"Unbelievable," Roy said, shaking his head. "They idol him so much that they will willingly hand over their only food?"

"Should we tell the captain?" Ferren suggested.

Roy thought for a moment. "No," he murmured. "I'm already on his bad side. You two don't need to be."

"Whatever you say," Charlie said finishing off his rations. "You gonna eat that?"

"Yes," Ferren and Roy said, continuing their meals straight-faced.

"Just trying to lighten the mood," Charlie murmured half-heartedly, dragging a stick through the sandy beach.

"Hey, look," Roy pointed towards the edge of the wood where several teams of cadets were setting up defenses. Walls made from huge, fallen trees, traps made by digging under the ground like a pitfall, and bunkers made from the palm leaves.

"Gentlemen, are you going to finish those?" An unmistakable voice brought the trio out of their gazing. They turned to see Tanner standing over them, several ration packs clutched in his greedy hands. As he saw their faces, his expression faded.

"Oh," he said to Roy. "It's you."

"Aye, it's him," Charlie stood. "Got a problem with that, mate?"

"Not at all," Tanner said with a grin and began to walk away.

"Wait," Roy called after him. He turned.

"Oh, so it can speak!"

"Drop it," Roy stood as well. "Just for now, and listen up."

"I'm listening."

"Alright then. Why?"

Tanner blinked then chuckled to himself. "The great question. Why anything, really? Why here, why now,"

"Shut it and answer him," Charlie glared at him with a gaze like ice.

Tanner rolled his eyes. "Why the rations, I assume?"

"Yep." Roy crossed his arms across his chest.

Tanner sighed dramatically. "As I've said before, we won't last more than a few more days here, especially with those blokes out there. When people start to realize that, they aren't going to want to sit around all day and wait for the inevitable. That need to take action. I've promised anyone who gives me their rations today will receive tenfold when we take action."

"Big words," Charlie said. "What, did you have to write on the back of your hand to remember them?"

"Cute," Tanner smirked. "Typical. No rations for any of you when I'm in power." He gave them one last sneer before turning towards another group of cadets and repeating his speech. Ferren groaned.

"What an ass," Charlie said as they sat back down.

"Agreed," Ferren added, finishing his rations. The label read *creamy potatoes.*

"Honestly, some people," Roy shook his head. "Whose sole purpose is being annoying."

"Ah!" A familiar voice called. "If it isn't Roy!"

"Speak of the devil," Charlie murmured as Doctor Lester Fitzroy came and sat beside him in his usual ivory coat and balding head. It was mostly ivory, anyways. Bloodstains now dotted the material.

"I think you'll be happy to know that Emily is doing just fine." The doctor smiled in an over an exaggerated way.

Roy stiffened, and he didn't have to look to feel the eyes of both Ferren and Charlie on him. "Good to know," he managed.

"Yes, isn't it?" the doctor beamed. "She wanted to convey to you her thanks for the way you so valiantly-"

"Yes, I understand. Tell her I said-" Roy heard Charlie snigger. He ignored him. "Tell her I said I was only doing my duty."

"So modest!" The doctor clasped his hands. "Truly the ideal officer!"

"Thank you, doctor." Roy almost growled, trying to change the subject. "So, do you have some time off from the medical lab?"

"If you could call some loosely tied hammocks a medical lab," the doctor suddenly grew melancholy. "At least I was able to stabilize most of their conditions. I wasn't able to save a couple of them."

"I'm sure you're doing your best, doctor," Roy assured him.

The doctor beamed. He simply adored compliments.

"Have you got your food yet?" Roy suddenly asked as an idea sprung to mind.

"Food? What kind?"

"They were able to salvage some lamb chops from the wreckage."

The doctor's face lit up. "Real lamb chops?"

"Almost," Roy said. "It's just over there." He pointed towards the ration crate.

"I might just have to get some!" The doctor rubbed his hands together feverishly as he began to stand.

"Good luck with your patients!" Ferren offered, but the doctor was long gone. Roy awkwardly turned to face the other two.

"Well, well, well," Charlie elbowed Roy playfully. "Miss Emily Ivy, eh?"

"Drop it," Roy warned.

Charlie chuckled. "The only woman on a ship full of two hundred guys and she falls for you."

"That's not what happened..." Roy stumbled over his words.

"Is it?" Charlie grinned.

Roy picked up a handful of sand threateningly. "Leave it alone."

"Alright, alright," Charlie laughed, holding his hands up in surrender, "Just picking on you, mate."

"Mm."

"What? I was!"

"Somehow, I don't quite-"

"Do we have any water?" Ferren suddenly interrupted, obviously having no interest whatsoever in their conversation.

The question took the two rather much by surprise. "Uh... Probably." Roy managed.

"No," Ferren shook his head. "None of them survived the crash."

"None?" Roy said. "What do we drink?"

"I think I can answer that," Charlie raised a hand as if requesting silence. "The captain mentioned that there were some trees with some kind of fuzzy brown rocks on them."

"That's great, but we still don't have anything to drink."

"Wait, I'm not done," Charlie waved a dismissive hand at him. "He mentioned some kind of milk being inside the rocks."

"Rocks with milk inside them?" Roy laughed. "Keep dreaming."

"I'll show you!" He stood as if going somewhere. "It's not even a ten-minute walk from here, near a kind of cove."

"If you think I'm following your mystical rocks on a wild goose chase-"

"Well, you are. Come on!" Charlie tried to pull them to their feet.

"Alright, alright," Roy stood willingly. "I'll come, but don't go crying to me when we figure out that they aren't real."

****

"Well, I'll be damned. They are real."

Not twenty minutes later, the trio stood before a huge palm tree, and at least six of Charlie's mythical rocks hung from it.

"Told you." Charlie crossed his arms.

"Hey, look at it from my perspective!" Roy turned to him. "You come to me with news of a rock with milk in it! It's a miracle we've found the rocks already, but now comes the real test."

"The inside?"

"Let's check out your little fantasy," Roy said, approaching the trunk.

"What are you doing?" Ferren stepped in front of him.

"I'm getting some rocks." Roy gently pushed him out of the way and wrapped himself around the trunk of the tree.

"You know what you're doing, mate?" Charlie asked. He actually sounded genuinely concerned.

"Of course!" Roy returned as he began to shimmy up the tree. "I climbed a wall that was centuries old! This should be..." He grunted from the effort. "Nothing!"

"Yeah, we all remember how that turned out," Charlie murmured.

"I heard that!"

"Evidentially so."

Roy rolled his eyes and continued his climb. It wasn't long before his hair brushed the bottom of the palm leaves. He looked up at the cluster of rocks.

Charlie and Ferren were right about them being fuzzy. A thin coating of hair sprouted around the edge. Roy drew his machete.

"I'm not too sure that's going to work," Ferren advised from below. "It looks like it's attached directly to the tree. Only a blast will get that off."

"Can I borrow a pistol?" Roy called back.

"Are we going to use a blast on this?" Charlie returned.

"We've got to settle this one way or another," Roy held his hand down. "Toss it up."

"Whatever you say," Charlie drew the broom handled weapon and lobbed it up. Roy watched it ascend and caught it by the barrel.

"Careful!" Ferren squeaked, and Charlie laughed. "What a way to go, eh?"

"Funny." Roy spun the weapon around and pointed it at the ligament between the rock and tree. He pulled the trigger and a shower of bark exploded around the impact point. He almost lost his grip, but the rocks were shaken free. Four of them fell to the ground.

"Nice!" Charlie caught one of them. "Come on down!"

Roy complied, sliding down the trunk until his feet hit the ground. "Now, for the moment of truth, eh?"

"Oh, I have no doubt." Charlie grinned and brought down the fuzzy rock on a large boulder. It cracked.

"Hah!" Roy pointed a finger at him. "Empty!"

But Charlie still looked satisfied. He turned the rock upside down, and a thick, white liquid flowed out.

Roy's spirits sank. "Really?"

Ferren cracked a smile as he split one of the rocks open as well. Carrying it tightly, he tilted it up and poured some of the liquid into his mouth. He quickly pulled it away, blinking rapidly.

"Very sweet," he said, and took another swig. "But good!"

"You're messing with me," Roy picked up one of the rocks and cracked it open. "It must just be undrinkable. You're faking it."

Charlie laughed, taking another gulp from his fuzzy drink. "Try it for yourself!"

Roy held his breath and took a sip. Sure enough, it was sweet, as the two insisted. "Unbelievable," he managed in between gulps. He hadn't had anything to drink in a long time. Not since they found the fort, and that fountain water was disgusting.

"I may assume he enjoys it," Ferren mumbled, and the two laughed.

"You assume correct," Roy set down his drink. "Come on, let's bring some back to the campsite."

The trio spent the next hour or so blasting the rocks off the trees in clusters. They used three blasts total, and had about seven or so left between Charlie and Ferren. After they had loaded themselves down the strange rocks, they began to make their way back to the others. As they walked, a small black bundle fluttered from Ferren's pocket and onto the ground.

"Hey," Roy stopped and picked it up. "Dropped this."

"Thanks," Ferren took it and studied it for a moment. "The schematics..." He murmured. "I was meaning to look over these."

"When we get back, eh?" Roy clapped a hand on his shoulder as Ferren returned the bundle to the chest pocket on his left side.

"When we get back..." Ferren suddenly got that long, faraway look that he would occasionally get when he would remember something he forgot. Roy knew it well.

"Remember something?" he asked.

Ferren shook his head. "No, no. Come on, let's hurry back."

Roy wasn't able to press the matter any further as Ferren ran ahead. Charlie eyed him warily.

"Long story," Roy murmured, falling into step with Charlie.

"About what?"

"His facial expressions can be rather... betraying at times."

"What do you think you saw?"

"He just looked like he... remembered something." Roy shrugged, lacking the proper way to describe it. "I don't know."

"Oh, it's fine." Charlie waved a hand. "As a matter of fact, an uncle of mine once-"

Charlie wasn't able to finish his story. For, in the distance, a gunshot fired. Then another. And another.

"What the hell?" Charlie said as they ran to catch up with Ferren. He was crouched behind a boulder, weapon in hand, paralyzed with fear.

"You alright?" Roy asked, crouching beside him.

"Fine," he murmured, his face pale. "Fine."

"Where did that come from?" Roy pressed as a few more gunshots rang out. Yelling could also be heard.

"The... camp..." He was barely able to it get out. Charlie and Roy nodded, and dropping their rocks, they continued down the way to the camp. Ferren was close behind. The sounds of fighting continued as they ran. It was about five minutes before the gunshots stopped, and they arrived at the edge if the woods. The trio crouched behind a few bushes. Together, they pushed the branches aside and peered through into their campsite. It was a disaster. The crew was lined up against the broken hull of the *Exodus*, their hands behind their heads, as at least two dozen armed pirates walked up and down the line, taking any weapons or valuables that they could find. Roy could see at least seven of their own crew dead.

"No," Ferren pulled his head away. "I can't look..." But Charlie and Roy were affixed to the spot. They couldn't have looked away if they wanted to. They saw the captain, beaten and bruised, in the line as well as Tanner, who didn't look much better himself. But something was different about him.

"Oh no," Charlie whispered. "Tanner. He has a gun." Sure enough, Tanner's hand was tingling towards his side, where a pistol lay concealed beneath his coat. A look of concentration was spreading across his face.

"That idiot," Roy hissed. "He's gonna do it. He's going to shoot."

"He'll get them all killed!" Ferren shrieked in horror. Charlie shushed him.

Tanner waited until the pirate nearest to him turned his back. He slowly pulled his coat aside, and Roy was clearly able to see the glint of metal on his weapon.

"Idiot!" Charlie hissed.

Tanner drew the weapon and, quick as a gunslinger, shot the pirate in the back. He howled in pain and backed off, dropping his weapon. Tanner made a dive for it, and for once, Roy didn't see any smugness on his face, but only determination, and confidence. This stunned Roy for a moment, and he momentarily forgot about his immense disliking for the boy. However, his choice was a rash one.

Tanner never reached the weapon. There were at least four pirates in range of him when he dove. They all raised their weapons.

Roy closed his eyes. He heard the guns fire, the blood splatter across the sand, and a thud. When he opened his eyes,

Tanner was there, on the ground, in a puddle of his own blood, smoke rising from the deadly weapons of the pirates. He was dead.

"NO!" Ferren screamed and, suddenly jumping to his feet, he pulled the trigger on his pistol once, twice, three times before the gun clicked and the slide locked. Empty. He hadn't even hit anything but sand and the *Exodus* hull.

Roy and Charlie tried to pull him down, but they were unsuccessful. Roy could almost feel the sights of the guns lock on him. Silently, he and Charlie raised their arms above their heads in a sign of surrender. Eventually, after throwing the empty pistol at the attackers, Ferren raised his arms as well, his hands in fists of rage. The armed pirates advanced towards them.

"Subtle," Charlie groaned. "Just great."

Ferren wasn't paying attention to either of them. "You lied," he said with a voice like venom. Roy was surprised to see him in such emotional chaos. Ferren was usually a very controlled, logic centered boy. His actions were clearly not logic centered. "You lied."

"What?" Roy blurted.

"We had an agreement!" Ferren pulled free of the pirate's grip, to receive a rifle stock to the shoulder. He allowed himself to be searched but continued speaking. "You said nobody would be killed. That you would just come in, look intimidating, and then take them off the island!"

"Ferren, what the hell are you talking about?" Roy hissed. "Don't be stupid!"

"I'm not being stupid! I..." He suddenly faltered. "I... look, I talked to them when we crashed, alright?"

"What?" Charlie joined in.

"Shut up!" Ferren practically screamed with rage. "Just... Listen! I was thrown from the ship during the crash, and I was hurt badly. They agreed to help me recover and that they would help the rest of us off this island if I just told them where we landed!"

"You did what?" Even the captain intruded on the conversation. "You can't be serious."

"I was acting for the greater benefit of the crew!"

"Greater benefit?" The captain spat, advancing toward him despite warnings from the pirates. "You couldn't honestly have believed them!"

"I... I don't know!" Ferren was having a tantrum. "I just don't know! They seemed so convincing and dedicated to putting our differences aside just for now...!"

One of the pirates pushed the captain back into line and pointed his rifle towards the trio. "In line."

Roy grimaced but advanced, standing beside Charlie and Ferren. If his arms weren't up, he would have elbowed him. Hard.

Then, there was a commotion behind them. Roy turned to see the doctor being pushed out of the *Exodus*, the barrel of a gun pressed against his back. He was arguing with a fierce intensity. "Those people will die without proper care!" he was saying. Roy could already see the spittle flying from his mouth with each protest. "I have to get back in there!"

"Keep moving." The pirate had no sympathy for the wounded crewmen.

"But they'll—"

"I don't care!" He pressed the gun harder. "Hurry up!"

"Their deaths will be on your hands!" Doctor Fitzroy said, pushing the gun away. "Do I look like a threat?"

"With this, you do." The pirate reached forward and pulled the pistol from Lester's holster at his side. "Armed?" He pulled the slide back, to reveal a full magazine. "And loaded. Planning a rescue?"

"What?"

"Now, now, now," one of the larger pirates approached the doctor. "Armed and loaded."

They were toying with him. Roy saw Ferren step out of the line. "Leave him alone!" he screamed.

The pirates seized the opportunity. They stepped towards him. "Who? The doctor?"

Ferren remained silent.

One of the pirates took a swing with the butt of his gun. It slammed into the side of Ferren's head, but still he said nothing. "Hey!" The doctor came up behind the pirates, and with a practiced hand, spun one around and hit him, hard, across the face.

The second pirate kicked the doctor in the stomach. "Get in line!"

Doctor Fitzroy spat some unkind words at the two thugs that even the captain flinched at before taking a place beside Roy. But the pirates weren't done with him. The one who the doctor hit raised his weapon and pointed it at him. Deep red blood trickled down his nose and around the corners of his mouth. The pirate beside him pushed the weapon down.

"We've killed enough of them," he criticized. "Let it go."

"Perhaps..." The brute's gaze turned down the line and halted on Ferren. A grin crept across his blood pasted face. "But him," he raised the weapon again. "He's served his purpose. We don't need him anymore. He would only be a witness."

The second pirate thought for a moment, before sighing heavily and shrugging his shoulders. "Just... fine. Fine, don't tell the boss."

Roy's eyes widened. "No, no, no," he said.

The pirate grinned and aimed his gun. "This is for the nose," he said.

Roy abandoned his spot in line and charged towards the pirate. At that point, he didn't care what Ferren had done. He was still a friend, and a friend that needed his help. All just a second too late. He saw the gun to off, and the blast casing clatter to the ground. He saw the silvery brass shimmer through the air, and he saw the blast hit Ferren just above the heart. There wasn't any blood that Roy could see; he hit the ground so fast.

Roy hit the pirate like a freight train, knocking him to the ground. He fell on top of him with his knees on his chest and clenched his fists and swung at his face, knocking him on the head with every ounce of strength he had left. It was only a few hits before he saw the blood splatter and felt the warmth of the liquid seep between his knuckles. Strong hands gripped him from behind, and he faced two strong brutes much like the one they killed at the fort. He felt hot tears on his face, as one of them raised their rifle, and brought it down on the side of his head. Everything went black.

Chapter Ten

Planning

"Hey! Kid!"

"Ugh..." Roy opened his eyes. The captain was looking down on him.

"You alright? Mulleary!"

"Am I...?" Images flashed through Roy's mind like a hurricane. *The dead crewmen. The pirates. Tanner. Ferren.* "Oh, God." He tried to push himself up. "Ferren. Ferren, is he-"

The captain was shaking his head. "They even took his body." He said in a reverent tone. "And Tanner's."

"...Did you trust him?" Roy asked after a moment of hesitation.

"Tanner?" the captain blinked. "Of course I did. He was one of my finest officers. Why?"

"No... nothing." Roy stood with some difficulty. "So, what happened? The last thing I remember, I was... Beating up the butt of a rifle with my face."

The captain chuckled slightly, his gray whiskers twitching. But there was still pain and disappointment in his eyes. "And you did a damn fine job of it, too."

"Mmm." was all Roy could say.

"After they killed Ferren, they took everything." The captain explained. "Weapons, ammo, supplies, food... We have nothing left."

"Not even the emergency rations?"

The captain shook his head. "Took every last pack."

"And they thought they were doing us mercy by leaving us alive." Roy rolled his eyes. "More like torture."

"But," the captain held up a finger. "They forgot something."

"Did they?"

"Come on, I'll show you."

They made their way over to the captain's makeshift tent. "I hid this behind the flap of the tent when they attacked," he pushed the tent flap aside, revealing three large crates, sealed with wax. "This was an experimental gunpowder that is more powerful in nature, but produces much more smoke when ignited. The academy and I managed to get a crate or two of it on board."

Roy could see where this was going. "So, if we light this up..."

"They wouldn't be able to see a thing." The captain clapped his hands together. "Their powerful weapons would be useless."

"Perfect." Roy took a seat with the captain at his table, easing himself into the chair. He was sore all over. "Now, we just need to find them."

"That, I might be able to help you with." Roy turned to see Charlie push the tent flap aside. "Forgive my intrusion."

"Not at all," the captain said. "So, you were saying...?"

"Right. When we went down, I got a glimpse of another crewmen's compass. I just had enough time to line it up with the ship that evidentially survived the crash." He pointed out the tent. "Southeast, that way. Just about near the other end of the island.

"That solves that." Roy murmured. "Now, how do we get there unnoticed? We can't just go in head first, it'd be suicide. And besides, we would need to put the gunpowder in the center of their camp to be most effective."

"As a matter of fact—"

"Wait, wait," Roy held up a hand. "Let me guess. You can help with that too?"

"Yep."

"Thought so. Go on." Roy folded his arms across his chest.

"Right," Charlie took a seat, uninvited. At that point, neither of the two cared. "Roy, remember the paper Ferren dropped on the way back from the fort?"

"Yeah..." The thought of Ferren made his heart drop.

"They were schematics. At least I think, if I remember my Latin classes. I wasn't able to get most of it, but from what I could understand, it explained how to get into a tunnel system."

"Tunnel system..." Roy echoed. *That would explain the middle-of-nowhere placement of the fort.*

"If I'm right, there's an exit from the caves along the coast, just about where the pirates are camped."

"That's perfect," Roy said, standing. "They'll be only lightly guarded there. They would never expect an attack from the puddle."

"Ocean," the captain murmured. "It's an ocean."

"The ocean," Roy corrected. "Yeah. Never expected from the... You know. Ocean."

"Right." The captain murmured.

"Yeah."

The silence was increasingly awkward until the captain clapped his hands together. "So, we'll set off as soon as we're ready."

"Aye, captain." Before they could salute, the captain shook his head.

"No, no, no," he said, "Not here. Here, I'm not the captain. A captain is no captain without a ship. Here, I'm Arthur, and that is how you will address me."

"Yes, si-" Roy hesitated. "Arthur." It felt awkward and inappropriate saying it, yet the captain seemed happy with it as he dismissed them and ordered a handful of crewmen to separate out the gunpowder into empty kegs found in the wreckage. Roy and

Charlie meandered outside, and neither said anything for a long while.

"I just..." Charlie finally said, sitting by a rock at the edge of the jungle. "I can't believe he's gone."

"Which one?" Roy said dryly, sitting beside him.

"Well, Ferren, mostly," Charlie replied. "I almost came to expect that from Tanner."

"Can you honestly say that?"

"What?"

Roy thought for a moment. "He just seemed so... Dedicated. When they killed him."

"What do you mean?"

Roy pursed his lips. "Just... You know. Even though he probably knew it was hopeless, he would rather have died than be taken as a prisoner."

"Do you know that for sure?"

Roy's anger spiked for a moment. "No. No, I don't." He turned to face him. "I just think that we've misjudged him somehow."

"Misjudged?" Charlie stood. "Misjudged? Roy, we're talking about the one who was planning a bloody mutiny. We're talking about the one who stole rations from mindless cadets who didn't know any better! You can't tell me we misjudged him!"

Roy stood to meet him. "He did what we didn't. He died for his people, his own crewmates!"

"He died because he was an idiot!" Roy could see the spittle flying from Charlie's mouth. "A moron! He was a backstabbing, overconfident, egocentric, and too washed up in his own vision of a perfect world to realize that he isn't invincible!"

Roy opened his mouth to shoot something - anything - back at him, but before he could, Charlie spoke up again, his voice in an anger-induced hiss. "Just like you."

Roy recoiled. His mouth hung open. He almost expected an apology, for Charlie to say that he didn't think before he spoke. But nothing came. Before any more insults were exchanged, Roy turned and walked over to the rest of the crew, who had gathered for their last stand. They had separated the experimental gunpowder into the kegs and were prepared to leave. Charlie joined Roy with them later, but both of them pretended not to notice each other. Before long, they set off.

*****

"Just through here," Roy instructed the crew, as he led them through the marsh to the fort they had discovered earlier. Charlie hung back behind them, with a seemingly remarkable interest in the plant life. Roy ignored him.

"Good God," the captain said as he pushed through the underbrush. "Who the hell would, in their right mind, build a fort in the middle of nowhere?"

"I'm not sure," Roy murmured. "But I'm not one to look a gift horse in the mouth."

"Mm." Arthur murmured in acknowledgment. They had just come over the edge of the valley and the fort was in sight.

"There it is." Roy advanced towards the gates, with the captain and crew in tow.

"Now that," Arthur said. "Is old."

"Is it entirely safe?" the doctor squeaked from behind them. Whether he was trying to be funny or not, nobody was laughing.

"Entirely," Roy assured him. He decided to leave out the incident with the wall.

"Good," doctor Fitzroy murmured behind him, not at all sounding convinced. "I think."

"Come on," the Captain said, gesturing for the crew to follow him. "Charlie, I hope you remember what those schematics said."

Charlie stepped forward, past Roy. "I think so, sir," he said. He, along with Roy and the crew, entered the fort through the front gate.

"Any idea where we start?" The captain said.

"Here," Charlie stepped towards one of the rooms. The room that smelled particularly bad.

"I would hold your breath," Roy advised, as Charlie approached it and flung the door open. The all too familiar odor of rotting flesh wafted from the room like death itself. Many of the crewmen wretched.

"Oh dear God," the doctor said nasally, with his hand on his nose. "You know, I think I'll wait outside. You know, keep watch." He scurried out of the fort.

"Is it really in here?" Roy asked Charlie. It was the first thing he had said to him since their heated discussion earlier. He said nothing in reply, only stepping further into the room.

"We'll need to move these," Charlie said, and the captain gestured towards a handful of cadets who seemed to be taking the situation rather well. They, along with Roy, stepped into the room and started carrying out the bodies. Each body needed two of them to carry it out. Roy took the legs of one along with a cadet. His—or at least, he assumed it was a he—his body was like sand. The decaying cloth around his legs fell apart almost instantly, exposing bare bone beneath. Roy coughed from the smell. He helped carry out three bodies until the room was empty. The old tiles of the walls were cracked, but bare, aside from a few old bloodstains blackened from age. No secret entrance, as far as he could tell.

"I don't see anything," Roy murmured just loud enough for Charlie to hear. He swore under his breath.

"This doesn't make sense," he said, kicking some fallen stones over with his boot. "It specifically said that there would be a door here."

"Maybe they were schematics for a different fort?" The doctor, who rejoined them after the bodies had been moved, suggested upon entering the room. Charlie shook his head.

"No, everything was the exact same!" He gestured to the walls around them. "Every detail!"

"Could there be some kind of trigger?" Roy dropped to his knees and felt around the floor for any kind of crack, or opening. *Nothing.*

"Maybe," he said. "But I can't find it."

"Did you see anything when you were here before?" Arthur asked.

"All we saw was the parchment, and we took that." Charlie offered.

"And the banner," Roy added, and as the words came out of his mouth, his head shot up and he locked eyes with Charlie for a moment. "The banner!"

They ran back to the room surrounded by tables, and to the spot where the shreds of the banner hung from rusted iron nails in the wall. Sure enough, a small stone button sat between the two nails.

"I can't believe I missed the thing," Charlie said as he pressed the button. There was a sound like stone grinding against stone, and some commotion from the room where they came from.

"Nice," Roy said, turning to Charlie. But he had already gone back in the other room. Sighing, Roy followed him there.

"Well, look at that," Arthur murmured, staring down at the floor. One of the floor tiles had slid aside to reveal an old climbing rope descending into an underground tunnel. "Well, let's get going," Arthur said. "Any volunteers?"

Chapter Eleven
Taking Action

Roy hit the ground first, his left foot sinking a good few inches into something mushy. "Ugh..." he murmured, pulling his boot loose with a loud sucking sound. He looked down the tunnel he landed in. It was surprisingly wide, with a glimmer of light at the end and patches of moss crawling up the walls. "It's safe!" he called up to the others. "Come on!"

Next came Charlie, then Arthur, and Doctor Fitzroy. They then began to help down the rest of the cadets. It took a solid hour for them to load into the cave since they could only go down one by one. Finally, they were all in the tunnel with the gunpowder, which was gently lowered, they closed the hatch above them, in case they were followed. The room was pitch black. One of the cadets found a torch alongside the wall and lit it, the fire casting eerie shadows along the walls. He looked at Arthur, who nodded.

Nobody spoke as they progressed down the hall. From time to time, Roy would look back at the remaining crew. They all had a certain fire in their eyes, a determination that no amount of firearms could hold back. Even the ones loyal to Tanner walked with a conviction, and a purpose. Even if he had died foolishly, Tanner provided them with a martyr, and a reason to fight.

Then, it clicked.

That was why he did what he did. Tanner made an idiot's move. He got himself killed for a hopeless cause. But, maybe he knew that. Tanner spent the entire time they had in the island gathering allies, and friends. He called it a 'mutiny', but Roy now knew that there was no intention of mutiny. Then, he died. Intentionally. He knew, since the second they landed, that he would, in the end, die. And he did. But, in doing so, he gave the hopeless cadets desperate enough to participate in a mutiny before even the first day had gone and passed, a reason to fight. A reason to keep living. And, in making enemies as well, he gave them something to inspire them. While someone's death, no matter how much you hate them, can be traumatizing, it can also brighten one's days when the person's presence is no longer a constant. Captain Arthur's words echoed in Roy's mind.

"He was one of my finest officers." Arthur had said to him that morning.

He sure was, Roy murmured to himself. *He sure was.* Roy clutched the torch a little tighter as they marched down the tunnel with a conviction. Despite how he despised him, Tanner had become Roy's martyr as well, whether he originally intended it or not.

"Roy," Arthur came up beside Roy. "I have something to ask."

"Of course."

"When we make it to the end of the island, we'll need three squads for each of the three barrels of powder," he explained, getting right to the point. "I'd like you to lead one of those squads."

"Yes, sir."

"No 'sir,' remember?" Arthur elbowed him playfully. "It's Arthur. And I'm asking you as a friend."

"Yes... Arthur." The words still felt awkward coming out of his mouth.

"That's more like it," Arthur clapped him on the shoulder. "And, ah, if you don't mind," he began to add in a low murmur. "I'm assigning the doctor to your squad. He seems to respect you."

"Of course." Roy wasn't as upset as he thought he should be. As annoying as doctor Fitzroy could be, he had grown on him during the past few days.

"Good. I'm assigning a cadet named Gulliver and Charlie as the other squad leaders." When Roy made a slight face, he added, "That won't be a problem, will it?"

"No, sir," Roy said loudly, hoping Charlie heard him. "Not a problem, sir."

"Good." he said, before turning off to talk to the others, leaving no comment about 'sir' this time.

They walked for a good two hours more. Roy's legs were sore and his arms ached from carrying the torch. It wasn't very heavy, but after a couple hours of holding it up, it felt like lead. Silently, Charlie came up to him and took it from him. "Thanks, mate." Roy murmured, but Charlie gave no indication he heard. Despite it being a kind thing to do, it was almost pointless. They had reached the end of the tunnel.

Water had begun to gather in puddles at their feet in cracks in the stone tunnel. Charlie extinguished the flame, for the light at the end of the tunnel now illuminated their path.

"Alright," the captain spoke up in a stage whisper voice. "We'll split up into our squads. Roy's, over here. Charlie's..."

They separated out into groups, and Roy, along with Lester Fitzroy, had five cadets. They were all first-years, and three of them were followers of Tanner, originally. They had a determination and a fire only his followers could have had. That was perfect.

Arthur came over to their group and called them outside the tunnel. The pirate camp wasn't five hundred feet from the exit of the tunnel, and it was well defended from the front.; bBut they were all around the backside of it. "Your squad will make their way there," he pointed towards a ramshackle building towards the middle of the camp. "Charlie's group will take the one closer to us, and Gulliver's will take the one towards the front."

"Should we wait until dark?" Roy suggested, thinking the smoke might not work with the added light. Arthur shook his head.

"The longer we wait, the more we risk detection," he countered, and Roy saw his point. "I, personally, feel the same way, but it's all too risky. They're expecting an attack from us, but the question is when."

"But they're also expecting a slaughter," Charlie added as he stepped up with his keg of powder in the strong arms of the cadets behind him. "They think they will win unconditionally, with their advanced weaponry. That's where we have the advantage."

"True," Arthur said, shouldering a fair sized club of driftwood over his shoulder. "And that's also why we need to act now. Are your squads ready?"

Roy glanced over to see his squad, including the fidgeting doctor, armed with sticks, rocks, clubs, and anything else they would find, along with the experimental powder.

"I think so." Roy stooped down to pick up a fair-sized chunk of rock just peeking out of the stream fed by the ocean.

"Then let's move," Arthur signaled for the cadets remaining behind, and they all crouched amidst the undergrowth. "You know your locations. Move out."

"Yes, sir." The three squad leaders said in a hushed undertone. For once, there was no argument from Arthur for the use of 'sir'. He saluted the squads, and crouched down with the rest. Roy clutched his chunk if stone tightly; he knew what had to be done. He didn't even need to give the order. He and the members of his squad moved as one, and even with the heavy powder keg, were almost completely silent. They moved together until they reached the edge of the pirate camp.

"Shh," Roy hushed his squad, as if they needed shushing. An armed pirate stood watch just before the bush they were crouched behind. Roy motioned to the cadets what to do, and they all nodded in understanding. He slowly crept towards the edge of the bush, his pulse pounding. He, himself, had never actually ended the life of anyone on the island so far, even during the skirmish at the fort. He had been lucky.

But no longer.

Before he could change his mind, he leapt up and caught the pirate in a neck hold. His eyes bulged in fear, and he opened his mouth to scream, but Roy had already dragged him back into the bush. In a flash, one of the cadets brought down a club with a mighty WHOMP onto the pirate's head. He stopped moving. Roy scrambled to pick up the pirate's gun. It was one of the pistols they had stolen from the Exodus during the attack.

Instinctively, he checked the pirate's pulse. He still had one. Somehow, he felt relieved.

The squad emerged from the bushes silently, and saw Charlie and his squad already at their location, with the keg propped up on crude, stick-stands and ready to go. They waited for the signal. Roy gave Charlie a nod as they passed by but never saw if he returned it as they went deeper into the enemy camp. It was very lightly defended towards the back end of the camp, but Roy and the others saw a significant increase in personnel as they advanced. They took out three more pirates along the way, and Roy specifically made sure they weren't killed. The concept of brutally ending one's existence hadn't seemed so grisly to him until after watching his comrades die.

As they progressed, they noticed the third squad, led by Gulliver, advancing more quickly than they were. It was a daring move, but since they had more distance to cover, it was understandable. It wasn't long until they reached the center of the pirate's camp, and the crude, slightly taller shelter Arthur designated as their target. Its two entrances on both the front and back were guarded by armed and fully alert pirates. Roy ground his teeth. This wouldn't be easy.

"Alright," Roy whispered as he turned to face his squad. "Here's the plan. You two will make it over to the bushes on the far side of the building, and-"

"The far side?" the doctor squeaked. "We'll go right through their line of sight!"

"I know, I know," Roy clenched his fists. "I'll figure it out, alright?"

"Figure it out?" the doctor said with firmness. "You had better figure it out within the few seconds it takes us to get out there, be seen and killed!"

"I'll... make a distraction," Roy pulled an idea out of the air. "I can throw a rock and—"

Roy didn't have time to finish his statement and probably make a fool of himself. A gunshot rang out in the distance. Followed by another, and another. Soon, the sound of several semi-automatic weapons firing at once chorused throughout the camp. But, just as quickly as it started, it was over. Roy looked over the bush to see weapon smoke rising in the distance, and the two guards at the doors had run off to join their friends towards the front of the camp; where Gulliver's squad had gone.

"Uh oh," the doctor murmured. "Was that-"

"Shh!" Roy said, pressing his hand over the doctor's mouth. The pirates were talking in the distance.

"These were the men from that ship." One of the pirates was saying. "The... whatever it was called."

"Didn't you see it?" another voice said. "It was painted in bright gold letters on the side of the hull!"

"I can't read." the first admitted shamelessly.

"Can't read? Come on, didn't you say you used to be in the academy?"

"I said used to. Why do you think I got kicked out on my ass?"

The first chuckled. "Ah, shut it. There's bound to be more of them around. Let's flush them out."

Roy stooped down to the others again. Gulliver and his entire squad were just killed. But they now had access to the building. "Let's go," Roy ordered without hesitation. "Before they come back."

The rest of the squad was either too shocked or too scared to question him. Even the doctor remained silent as they moved out into the open and towards the entrances of the ramshackle shelters. Roy got to the forward facing entrance first and held the flap open for the two cadets struggling with the powder keg. The veins in their arms bulged as they made their way inside and set the keg down as quietly as they could, with a sigh of relief. Once they were inside, Roy joined them and let the flap close.

"What are we going to do without Gulliver's squad?" The doctor finally spoke up after what seemed like an eternity. "We'll only cover a little over half the camp with what we have left!"

"It'll have to do," Roy said and drew his newfound pistol, holding the broom handle weapon tight in his hand.   "Light it."

The cadets didn't argue as they struck a flint across one of the rifle's barrels. The keg sparked and caught after only a few strikes.

"Uhh, how big will this explosion be?" the doctor suddenly asked. By then, the fuse was already half burned.

Roy hadn't even considered it himself. He soon realized that this was a poor choice. "Everybody out!" he exclaimed, abandoning their original stealthy approach, they flung the flap open and tumbled out into the open air. He heard several pirates yell in fright, and looked up to see three burly men with guns aimed at their squad. Roy closed his eyes and threw himself onto the ground. The resulting explosion was deafening. It completely blew the shelter apart, and a massive cloud of black smoke blasted through the camp like a storm of blasts. Roy brought his head up and saw absolutely nothing. The powder was obviously extremely effective.

Over the sound of surprised gunshots and screams, Roy heard a pirate barking orders. "To arms! To arms! Rally the men, and be snappy about it!" he was screaming. Roy pushed himself to his feet and stumbled along, holding his hands out in front of him like a blind man. The voice drew closer as he forged through the sea of darkness until he was almost on top of the surprised pirate.

As soon as he was able to see him, Roy lunged forward and slammed the butt of the pistol into the man's chest. He dropped his weapons as bones cracked and he was flung back into the door of a shelter. The door shattered like glass and the two of them fell into the ramshackle building, Roy on top of the pirate. It only took a couple more well-aimed strikes around the head to silence him.

Roy pushed the man's unconscious body away and stood up. The smoke hadn't affected the shelter as much, but it still greatly reduced visibility. He was only just able to make out the shape of a stunned, older-looking boy at the other and of the shelter. Roy was on him in an instant, forcing his elbow against the pirate's neck and back into the wall. He pressed the barrel of his gun against the worn flight academy uniform and the trigger was halfway depressed until he realized who he was looking at. Roy was stunned as he stared at his old friend, who stared back at him in relatively the same way. The two locked eyes.

"What?" Was all Roy could say to the boy he had at gunpoint. He almost shot Ferren; who seemed pretty alive at first glance. Roy pulled back, lowering his gun. "You're alive?" he asked in awe.

"Of course I'm alive!" Ferren snapped. "But how are you alive?"

"I saw them shoot you," Roy continued, almost ignoring Ferren. "You were dead! How are you here?"

Ferren's eyes glinted with a certain deviousness. "Oh, you'll love this." He reached into his shirt pocket and pulled out the thick letter they found in the fort; It had a blast stuck in it.

"No way," Roy said, his jaw dropping.

"Yep." Ferren tossed him the letter, which was oddly weighted due to the blast. Roy caught it and examined it. It was the real deal, alright.

"I don't believe it," Roy said jokingly. "Old William Baker took a blast for you?"

"So it would seem." Ferren took the letter back.

"But wait," Roy added, only just registering what he said before. "What do you mean? How am I alive?"

"They told me-" Ferren's voice faltered. "They... told me you were all dead." He said finally, in just barely a whisper. "That me, along with a few others, were the only survivors."

"Well, they lied," Roy said. "And we're here to help you guys and take back what they stole from us. Including a steam cell."

"The cell!" Ferren exclaimed with a certain element of excitement. "I know where they're keeping it! It's toward the front of the camp!"

Roy winced. He was afraid Ferren was going to say that. "That's the one place we aren't going to be able to get to easily."

"Why?"

"The squad we sent to light the smoke powder at the front end of the camp was killed."

Ferren grimaced. "How many?"

"Only about seven, maybe eight. I didn't count."

"I see."

Roy paused a moment. "Well, we're wasting our time here. Come on!" He stooped down to pick up the pistol the pirate he took down was armed with, and after checking to ensure it was loaded, tossed it to Ferren. He caught it and holstered it at his belt before continuing outside with Roy.

The battle had escalated. The *Exodus* crewmen had obviously gained an advantage, as the majority of the bodies were that of pirates. But most of the smoke from the two explosions had cleared, and nobody was remaining in their location.

"They must be at the front," Ferren suggested, and the two sprinted towards the front of the camp. It didn't take long to get there, and the situation was exactly what they were originally trying to avoid.

It had broken out to a firefight. Shelters had been torn apart or overturned to act as barriers for the incoming storm of blasts. The two sides had taken up defensive positions, and a no-mans-land was present for about twenty meters before the pirate's defenses began. It was littered with corpses and blood. It repulsed both Roy and Ferren, but they knew that stopping to think about it now would get them both killed. They scrambled towards the *Exodus* defenses and crouched behind an overturned shelter next to the captain, who had joined the fight.

"Roy! Good to see you're okay." Arthur said, and then noticed Ferren. "And... you?"

"It's a long story, s-... Arthur." Roy corrected himself. "But the basics of it are that we thought he was dead, and he's not."

"Got it."

"Have we made any advancement at all?" Ferren inquired.

"None," Arthur said flatly. "It's been like this for the past ten minutes, and it doesn't look like it will change soon."

"Damn it." Roy cursed. "This was exactly what we were trying to avoid in the first place!"

"I know, but there's nothing to be done about it now."

"Captain! Roy!" A familiar, squeaky voice exclaimed, as doctor Fitzroy scrambled beside them. "Good to see you made it."

"You as well, doctor," Arthur said.

"I think I have a way through this," the doctor said; he practically had to yell to be heard over the gunfire. "The enemy's defenses are crude, and one of them, towards the left, is only a tarp. If someone could get through there, we could flush them out!"

"I would if I could, but there's no way to get through the grounds in between with ought being blown to pieces!" the captain exclaimed as he fired a few shots from his rifle towards the enemy.

"You can leave that to me," Charlie said as he joined them. He held not one, but two of the enemy's modified semi-automatic rifles. "I can give you cover."

"Thanks, mate," Roy said. He had no intention of holding a grudge here.

"I take it you'll be going?" Ferren asked Roy.

The thought had occurred to him, but he was expecting it. "Yes, I will."

"Be careful," Ferren said in a surprisingly comforting tone for the usually emotionless lad. But before Roy could leave, Charlie planted a hand on his shoulder.

"Listen," he said impatiently. "I know you're busy, so I'll keep this quick. I, personally, don't give a damn about what you thought of Tanner. And I don't want that to affect our friendship or our career. If you want to respect him, fine. If not, go for it. Just know that I've got your back with this one, mate."

Roy gave him a genuine smile. "I appreciate it." Charlie nodded, and then raised his two weapons. "Covering fire!" he heard him shout, and several gunshots erupted from the side of the *Exodus* crewmen.

Roy knew that was his chance. Clutching his pistol tight, he placed a hand over the crude wooden defenses and vaulted over it. Sure enough, the pirates had ducked behind their barricade to avoid the new storm of blasts. Roy ran through the dirt and leaped over bodies and craters in the ground, likely from grenades. His heart pounded; he kept his eyes locked on the pirates. If even one of them decided to take a blind shot from there, he was dead. Thankfully, none of them did. Roy reached the tarp and, not slowing down, dropped to his knees and slid under it. He emerged from the other side, pistol raised and ready to fire.

There were five pirates on the other side. They only just noticed him and, shouting a few curses, raised their weapons. But Roy never gave them the chance.

Mindlessly, numbly, he pulled the trigger. Once, twice, three times. He lost count. Before he knew it, the pistol was empty and five fresh corpses lay on the ground before him. Roy lowered the weapon. The tip of the barrel was red-hot from the rounds he fired in such quick succession. He looked around and counted five empty blast casings in the dirt. Five shots, five kills.

All of the gunfire had ceased. Roy shakily pushed himself to his feet, to see his comrades, including Charlie, the doctor, Ferren, and captain Arthur. Charlie reached him first, leaping over the barricade and catching him in a bear hug.

"We did it, mate," he said, holding him by the shoulders. "We bloody did it! The cell's ours, the pirates have surrendered, and we won!"

"We won..." Roy said in a daze. "What a victory."

"We won! We won!" was all Roy was able to hear. He looked down at his hands.

All he could see was the blood of other men.

Chapter Twelve

Conclusion

The crew gathered the supplies, and everything else they could find that might be useful; guns, ammunition, the steam cell needed to get them off the island and even their ration packs, still unopened and untouched. Roy enjoyed a 'pork roast' on his way back to the *Exodus*. He walked in a daze, with naught but Ferren and Charlie at his side. He spoke up.

"I killed five men." He said, out loud, to nobody in particular. "Five men."

"Roy..." Charlie, said, putting, put a hand on his shoulder. "You did what had to be done."

"I know, it just..." Roy stumbled over his words. "Shocked me that I didn't even have to think twice."

"It was them or you, mate." Charlie drew his hand back. "And if you hadn't done what you did, a lot more men, who were innocent, would have died."

"I suppose you're right." Roy smiled a little. "How about a few coffees when we get back, yeah?"

"I wouldn't be against it," Ferren said. For the first time since the battle... they laughed.

It was dark out by the time they returned to the *Exodus'* wreckage. Cheering and celebrating, the crew got back onto the ship, and a crew of engineers went below deck to install the steam cell. As Roy made his way up to his assigned quarters, he bumped into the doctor.

"Doctor," Roy said to him with a smile as they passed.

"Ah! Roy!" The doctor turned to walk beside him. "I thought you would like to know that Miss Ivy has made an almost complete recovery and is up and about!"

"Good to hear!" Roy said, and then added, "The pirates left her alone?"

"I managed to conceal her when the pirates came. To their knowledge, this was a ship full of men."

"Good." Roy hesitated. "She... didn't happen to mention me to you at all, did she?"

"No, not to my knowledge." The doctor shook his head with a frown. "Any reason?"

"No. No reason." Roy shook his head, but internally, he was relieved. It would have been very awkward for the next several days if she had.

"Alright then," the doctor said rather awkwardly, and then he stopped at the next corridor. "This is where I'll be leaving. If you need anything at all, give me a call. I hear the communications relays are operational again. And... get a good night's sleep, Mister Mulleary." He gave Roy a kind smile. "You've certainly earned it."

"Thank you, doctor." Roy extended his arm and shook the doctor's hand firmly. "Good night, doctor."

"You as well." They parted ways down their separate corridors.

Roy was relieved. Emily Ivy had been a little too close for his liking. And besides, with her at his side, half of the young men in the flight academy would have pounded him into a pulp. He chuckled to himself. *How things work out, eh?*

Not three corridors after the doctor's unexpected meeting, Ferren turned a corner and fell into step with Roy. "Are you near quarters 3-A?" he asked abruptly.

"I'm in quarters 3-A, Ferren," Roy said with a laugh. He was sure this was the captain's doing. "It seems we'll be bunk buddies again."

"That is evident." Ferren showed no sign of happiness. "I want to apologize."

"Apologize? For what?"

"I lost my will when the pirates took my hostage, both times. I never should have told them the things I did, or given them our location. I just couldn't do away with the feeling that I was afraid. That they would find a way to kill you instead..."

"Ferren," Roy clapped a hand on his shoulder. "I don't need the speech. We're friends. I don't care what you've done, or who you've sold information to. We're friends. Got it?"

"I... got it," Ferren said in agreement. "Thank you."

"Anytime."

They turned the corner to a door marked 'crew quarters, 3-A'. "This is the place," Roy said, opening the door and stepping inside along with Ferren. The place was wrecked. The table and chair were overturned, and something ceramic had been smashed to dust. The only things still in place were the mattresses and the bunks, conveniently bolted to the floor. Roy looked over at Ferren, and the two locked eyes. A wicked grin spread over their faces, and without saying a word, the two dashed for the bunk. Ferren got there first and threw himself on top, but Roy wasn't far behind. He climbed up with him, and the two began to wrestle for the top bunk. Despite the fact that Ferren was older, Roy still had the strength advantage and was able to throw him from the bed with little effort. Ferren landed with a thud on the lower bunk and laughed. For the first time in what seemed like years, but was actually just days, he laughed.

Roy laughed along with him.

And they both knew that nothing had changed between them.

THE EXODUS PROJECT A.J. ROWE

A. J. ROWE

     A.J. Rowe is a resident of Birmingham, MI, and a sophomore at University of Detroit Jesuit High School. He has been writing creatively since he was thirteen years old and enjoys reading and writing novels of the fantasy/fiction genre.

     When he is not writing, he enjoys tennis, golf, chess and working on his Eagle Scout rank in the Boy Scouts of America. A.J. is a member of his high school ping pong club and *Inscape* editorial staff and is considering a career in professional writing and teaching.

     Like any writer, he is always working on his next novel.

www.ingramcontent.com/pod-product-compliance
Lightning Source LLC
Chambersburg PA
CBHW072002170626
46813CB00005B/1969